One More Time

Damien
LEITH

One More Time

A NOVEL

HarperCollins_Publishers_

Visit Damien Leith's website:
www.damienleith.com.au
www.myspace.com/damienleith

HarperCollins*Publishers*

First published in Australia in 2007
by HarperCollins*Publishers* Australia Pty Limited
ABN 36 009 913 517
www.harpercollins.com.au

HarperCollinsPublishers
25 Ryde Road, Pymble, Sydney, NSW 2073, Australia
31 View Road, Glenfield, Auckland 10, New Zealand
77–85 Fulham Palace Road, London, W6 8JB, United Kingdom
2 Bloor Street East, 20th floor, Toronto, Ontario M4W 1A8, Canada
10 East 53rd Street, New York NY 10022, USA

National Library of Australia Cataloguing-in-Publication data:

Leith, Damien, 1976– .
   One more time.
   ISBN: 978 0 7322 8641 5.
   I. Title.
A823.4

Cover design by Matt Stanton
Cover images: Girl with guitar and man walking courtesy Getty Images;
   fabric and the mountains courtesy Shutterstock
Author photograph by Christopher Morris © 2007 SONY BMG MUSIC
   ENTERTAINMENT (AUSTRALIA) PTY LIMITED
Typeset in 11.5/18 Sabon by Kirby Jones
Printed and bound in Australia by Griffin Press
70gsm Bulky Book Ivory used by HarperCollins*Publishers* is a natural, recyclable
product made from wood grown in sustainable forests. The manufacturing processes
conform to the environmental regulations in the country of origin, Finland.

5 4 3 2 1   07 08 09 10

To the loves of my life,
Eileen, Jarvis and Jagger

1. Mani Lama

Two-door cars never make for a grand entrance, especially for the person in the back, and after a moment of fumbling to find the latch under it, the front passenger seat flew forward and a man surfaced from the car. I could hardly believe my eyes.

There was no way he'd be able to carry my bag!

'This is my cousin Mani Lama. He will be your trekking guide.'

Dressed in a pair of combat trousers, worn-out white trainers and a plain black t-shirt, Mani looked no taller than four feet, and was as thin as an average twelve-year-old. Tiny. His leathery brown skin marked a life outdoors, and although he looked relatively young, his closely cropped hair was greying. How could he guide me up some of the steepest slopes in the world?

Mani reached out and greeted me with a firm handshake. His manner was strict and teacher-like yet I felt a little anxious as I returned his grip and wished him good morning.

'Will you be able to carry this backpack?' I asked, describing with my hands what I meant.

Mani seemed surprised by the question. 'Easy!' he replied. Obviously he understood me. That was good. Mani was confident and so perhaps I should be too.

'I promised to you that I would get you good man and here he is. If you have any problem, Mani will help you. Now enough talking, I think it is time to leave! You enjoy trek. Taxi will take you to starting point at Nayapul. I will see you when you finished!'

Cousin Om was straight to business — just as he had been when I'd entered his trekking shop, the day after I arrived at Pokhara, still dazed and confused after the 24-hour bus ride from the Indian border.

'You have to go to Pokhara, it's heavenly.'

Her words had never left my mind, and a month after she'd spoken them, I'd taken her advice. The chances of meeting up with her there were slim, but secretly a part of me hoped it would happen.

Pokhara was indeed heavenly. The small town, lush and green with surrounding forest, nestled quietly beneath the towering snow-capped Annapurna Mountains. The air felt clean, the streets and shop fronts looked quaint, and a general sense of contentment seemed to reside amongst the locals.

On the calm waters of Fewa Lake, tourists paddled in rented canoes, and locals fished from its grassy banks. In the centre of the lake was a small island, scantily treed and home to an old temple. Temples are common in Nepal but this was the first one I'd seen in such an idyllic location.

I was keen to explore Pokhara, but on that first day I decided instead to take some time to unwind and relax. I lay back on a grassy patch on the bank. The sky was a brilliant blue and, in contrast to the lake, dazzlingly bright. I closed my eyes and listened: a mish-mash of sounds, all of them soothing, none of them threatening.

Om's trekking shop was the one nearest to my hotel and it was when I passed it that I got the idea to withdraw further from the chaos of life and go right up into the mountains — away from people, away from responsibility. I'd never undertaken anything as strenuous before but it was just the retreat I needed — bracing, cleansing.

Over the course of an hour one day in Om's trekking shop, he managed to part me of five thousand rupees for a guide-porter and six thousand rupees for the clothing and equipment he insisted I'd need. I bought everything he told me to buy. Boots, water canister, rain-proof clothing, sleeping bag. He even chose the type of trek I should do — a ten-day round trip to the Annapurna Base camp.

Now standing in front of the small blue taxi, which periodically coughed black smoke and seemed a little too heavy for its flattish-looking tyres, Om was firmly directing affairs again. It was important to begin early, he insisted. It looked like it was going to be a hot day and walking in such heat would be gruelling.

Heaving the backpack in front, Mani and I squeezed behind it into the back of the taxi and gave a final glance towards Om, who briskly waved farewell. Then, with introductions to our driver, Umesh, over, the taxi pulled off in the direction of Nayapul.

For the next ten days I was going to do something many others only dream of. This is what life is all about, I thought. Taking the chance that's offered us. The weather was sensational, I was reasonably fit, and whatever Mani lacked in physique he seemed to make up in confidence — everything was just perfect!

* * *

Suddenly the traffic came to a standstill.

'Roadblocks, they are everywhere now in Nepal!' Umesh explained as he wound down his window and began to gesticulate like all the other drivers ahead of us. 'You know about the Maoist?' he went on in good English.

I had heard about the Maoists but I could tell from his tone that he intended on teaching me more.

'The Maoist fight for the poor people of Nepal. You know that we still have our King Gyanendra? But he is not interested in government.' Umesh's tone became fiery, more intense. 'Politics in Nepal is nothing but arguments between the king and the government and all the time it is the poor people who suffer.'

He looked to Mani for confirmation but Mani didn't appear to understand quite what he'd said and acknowledged him with a confused smile. We advanced to second place in the roadblock queue.

People had warned me about the Maoists before I'd left for Nepal. The leader of the Maoists was a man commonly known as Prachanda, meaning 'the fierce one' — apparently he was something of a ghost, rarely seen or photographed, forever in hiding. In their early days, I knew, the Maoists had been seen as the hope of the indigenous people of Nepal. But the government hadn't taken their small faction seriously. Now, ten years down the track, the Maoists were supposed to number more than fifteen thousand and be heavily armed. The Maoists had become a force to be reckoned with.

'If Prachanda orders for all businesses to strike, then that is what will happen. He has the government frightened and nobody wants bombings!'

Bombings? I wasn't aware of any bombings, and Umesh could see that their mention disturbed me.

'Yes, bombings! Prachanda has bombed government, even royalty. The last time that he ordered a strike in Kathmandu, he attacked and bombed businesses that didn't do as he told. It is a very bad situation — and now it involves tourists too.'

I'd read up on Nepal's history in a guide book in India before coming, but I could see it was the present-day activities that I should have looked into.

'They will approach you in the mountains while you trek. They will be heavily armed! They will want money from you, a donation.'

'But that's crazy,' I growled, 'A donation is something you give because you want to, not because you're being threatened.'

'It's not so bad,' Mani interrupted, apparently now

following the conversation. 'Maoist no harm, they common man with family. No problem.'

'It doesn't sound like no problem,' I persisted.

'You no worry,' replied Mani with ease.

We reached the head of the queue. The sight of five soldiers in combat gear armed with machine guns unnerved me. The elation I had felt as we set off had dampened. Now, despite Mani's assurances, I felt doubtful, pensive. In fact, what did I know about Mani and Umesh in any case? They could both be dangerous terrorists for all I knew.

The soldiers stopped the car and asked Mani and the driver to get out.

Dear Holy God —

Through the backseat window I could see one of them take some papers from Mani and study them. Then a new thought occurred to me: I hoped they wouldn't take it into their heads to have some fun with us. I recalled my last incident with officials when I crossed the Indian border into Nepal.

'Fill in this form,' the Indian immigration officer had grunted.

I had riffled through my bag for a pen but I knew already that I didn't have one. It was mid-afternoon and the scorching heat was draining in.

'Have you got a pen that I can use?' There was one in his hand.

'No, you must use your own.'

'I don't have one.'

'What can I do, you must have your own. This is not my problem.'

'But I don't have one.' My voice was becoming louder. 'Can I not borrow yours?'

'I need mine right now. Maybe you should look through your luggage once again. Under this bright sun maybe your eyes are not so good.'

It was monsoon season in India, and the streets were mucky with scattered puddles and nowhere for me to lay my backpack down. This was absurd, I thought.

'You know what? Keep your pen. If it's that bloody well precious to you. I wouldn't want it anyway.'

'Sorry, I cannot understand a single word that you are saying. Can you speak English?'

I'd felt tiny, stupid and infuriated.

One of the soldiers at the checkpoint moved towards the car and leant in the door. I moved to get out from the back. 'No please, sir, stay.'

It surprised me. For all he knew I too could be a Maoist sympathiser smuggling weapons to the enemy.

I sat back while two soldiers made a brief inspection of the car's interior.

All satisfactory, it seemed, and a few minutes later we were on the road again, although Umesh continued to peer into his rear-view mirror. I looked back as well. The roadblock was a depressing sight in a country otherwise so blessed with natural beauty. Although the soldiers had been polite and unthreatening, it was confounding, as always, to be held up and searched by men with guns.

Not until the roadblock had disappeared did Umesh relax. He turned on the radio, maximum volume. Craning round to Mani and me as he drove, he shouted, 'No more roadblocks. This music is good, yes?'

It was six o'clock in the morning and pounding through our humble little car now came the haunting sound of a Nepalese folk tune: sitars, bongo drums and a foreign musical scale. The use of so many minor notes in a popular duet was discordant to my ear.

The trip to Nayapul would take us more than an hour, Om had told me, but Umesh must have taken his morning dose of speed. To the accompaniment of the blaring music, he set about gaining pole position on the narrow dirt road. We swerved monkeys, dodged buses, skidded past people on bicycles and honked the horn at fellow lunatic taxis, and I felt my hands clutching for dear life to the base of my seat.

As the road wound higher and more precipitous, the traffic thinned, allowing Umesh to speed up further. Torn between viewing the plunging drop down the mountainside — towards which we veered all too frequently — and oncoming lorries forcing us to give way on the narrow road. I shut my eyes.

'*Dear Holy God, please protect* —' massive swerve — female vocalist shriek — need to start again.

'*Dear Holy God, please protect Mam, Dad* —' another swerve — my thumbs not aiming in an upward direction — need to start again.

'*Dear Holy God, please protect* —' didn't feel right — had to start again.

'*Dear Holy God* —'

'It's okay? You happy?' Umesh asked, taking his eyes off the road again to catch my eye.

I took a deep breath and struggled to reassure him. My lungs filled, my chest rose. *You can do this!* I thought. But it was useless. The prayer hadn't been said correctly and we wouldn't be safe until it had. I took another deep breath, this time holding it for a short while before finally releasing it with a gasp.

Dear Holy God, please protect Mam and Dad, John, Sarah and Sam, Benji and Rusty, all my friends and relatives and everybody who needs your help today.

On that journey to Nayapul, perfection was elusive. The erratic driving, pounding music, conversation, my own early morning tiredness, all conspired to make forming the perfect prayer near impossible.

I caught myself muttering out loud and darted a guilty look at Mani. Had he heard me? Perhaps the music was a blessing. If he'd heard something he didn't let on.

But day one had moved on to the wrong mental foot for me.

2. Registration

Mani and I stood on the edge of the road and watched the taxi speed away from us, the pounding music dissipating to a gentle hum and then finally nothing. It was very quiet.

Umesh had completed the drive to Nayapul well within the predicted hour, even though the route had wound steadily uphill for most of that time. While we drove, towering trees had surrounded us in every direction and when the taxi had finally come to a halt and Umesh had plonked us down, we were in the depths of the forest. Other than a few rickety food stalls on the side of the main road, Nayapul was nothing but a gateway to the trekking path.

Mani occupied himself with my backpack.

'Sorry if it's too heavy,' I said ineffectually.

'No problem, it's only little bit heavy,' he acknowledged with a cheerful nod, and within moments he had the bag on his shoulders.

'We go Birethanti first and then some breakfast. You little hungry, maybe need eat now?' He looked at me cagily.

I was starved. 'No, I'm fine for now,' I answered. I figured that it was best to make a start sooner rather than later, and walking on a full stomach would probably just slow my progress. Mani turned away from me and took the first steps of our journey together.

Ah, I thought, here we go!

With the food stalls behind us, Mani led the way to a steep embankment not far away. We climbed down the embankment and reached an even, stony path. Within minutes the Nayapul road was behind us and out of sight, replaced by beautifully lush and vibrant countryside. It felt exciting: heading into the unknown, shaking off the anxiety of the speeding taxi and giving in to a sheer sense of release. Not as dramatic as when I'd upped and left Ireland, but similar.

The morning air was cool, its taste crisp and clear. Vibrant colours caught my eye, and I hungrily absorbed the sights and smells and sounds. Though it wasn't windy, the gentle sway of the trees shushed over the sounds of cattle grazing nearby and distant voices of people starting their day. A sweet, pleasant scent filled the air, surprising, as most of the intermittent clearings were used for farming.

Surrounded by huge trees and a deep undergrowth of greenery I felt invigorated. Everything was so close and so present — not so different from landscape that I'd experienced before, but with a unique and indescribable feeling in the air, as though I'd stepped back in time.

The walk to Birethanti was gently downhill for the most part. Advancing down the terraced foothills, snippets of history were revealed in every direction. The mountainsides of Nepal had looked like they'd barely changed since the days long ago when trekkers first discovered their wonders. We passed through tiny villages and were greeted with curious, cheerful eyes and the optimistic Nepali welcome, *Namaste*. Even small children hailed our arrival with sweet and high-pitched *namastes* a hundred times over, as we walked past them. It was difficult to comprehend the hardship I knew lay within this world; the children all seemed oblivious to it, carefree.

'You don't know how good you have it,' my mother would say with a raised finger pointed in my direction. 'Think about the poor children in Africa!'

The authoritative finger was a good move and Mam always knew just when to use it. When I was very young the raised finger was one step away from getting smacked and despite the fact that the smacking stopped as I got older, the fear remained. If Mam raised her finger, we all listened. And here, in the last few minutes I had observed many young children taking responsibility for their siblings while their parents worked all day — children as young as ten, carrying younger brothers or sisters on their backs. Mam would be satisfied with this lesson.

Mani suddenly stopped and waited for me to catch up. 'We eat here.' He gestured towards a small village visible ahead. We had been walking for just over thirty minutes and had reached Birethanti.

Once in the village, Mani found us a humble little home that doubled as a 'teahouse.' He was quietly welcomed by an overworked-looking young woman who discreetly turned away from my view. Disappearing behind a screen, she re-emerged with a man — her husband, I presumed. The man welcomed Mani heartily in Nepali, casting pleased looks in my direction. It was obvious how important guides such as Mani were to the sustenance of the villages along the trekking route.

'*Namaste,*' the man said to me. 'You like milk tea? Yes? Yes?'

I ordered some milk tea and some Tibetan bread, which I had never tasted before.

'Good food. We have very good food. And you have very good guide,' he said, slapping Mani over the shoulder. 'Like a brother to me,' he continued. 'Very strong.'

He left to prepare the morning meal. 'Yes, you get good food here,' Mani said. 'Many, many teahouse in Birethanti,' he went on. 'Everybody make their home place to eat and place to sleep for tourist. If they are lucky tourist will stay with them. But here the best.'

While we waited for our food to arrive Mani excused himself and slipped out of sight. I sat contentedly at the table and enjoyed the beauty of my surroundings.

We were located in the centre of the village and from where I sat, I had a great view of everything. It reminded me of a tourist village named Glendalough back home in Ireland. Famed for its eighth-century monuments, Glendalough was one of the most inviting places in Ireland. I think it was the timelessness of both places that made them seem similar to me: both had stone houses, small and practical, bundled together in close proximity and cobbled pathways throughout. A sense of little having changed since people first put up dwellings there hung over each place.

I remembered a summer day in Ireland when Dad had packed us all into the rusting blue Datsun Cherry and driven the whole family to Glendalough. The sun was shining for a change, we all ate ice cream — what more could a car full of kids want? I remembered how my brother John had got saturated after slipping into a nearby rock pool. Dad hung John's trousers out the car window as we drove so that they would dry, and somewhere between Glendalough and home they came loose and vanished!

But at twenty-eight, I was long past family outings and ice-cream cones, even though the memories were as happy and fresh as if it had all been only last week.

Maybe I'm starting to miss home, I thought. Or perhaps the guilt was beginning to set in.

'You have nothing to worries about!'

Mani startled me. He'd reappeared unexpectedly and I jumped a little.

He grinned wildly.

'You've changed your clothes?' I said.

He had replaced his trousers and t-shirt for a pair of faded blue shorts and light hoody-styled top. He regarded me quizzically; perhaps I'd spoken too fast for him to understand.

'It is Nepali fighting with Nepali,' he replied, to my confusion. 'They like tourist, not want harm tourist.'

'Who? What are you talking about?'

'The Maoist! They only fight with Nepali. If I wear combat — you know combat?'

I had to think for a second. 'Ah yeah, you mean like army clothes?'

'Yes!' He was pleased I understood. 'Like army. If I wear combat then Maoist they are shooting at me, maybe make me dead-ed. But if I look like guide-porter, no problem.' Mani ended his sentence with a questioning pout, his large lower lip slightly overlapping his upper.

He had been fidgeting while he spoke and there'd been a nervous tremor in his voice, so I guessed his words of reassurance were not entirely for my benefit. No doubt in his life he'd witnessed his fair share of crazy things but the Maoist threat was new territory. The assurance that he'd shown in the taxi, I noticed, was receding a little now we were actually in the mountains. Clearly the Maoists did worry him.

'Do you think that we will meet them?' Mani's

anxiety was a little contagious. 'The taxi driver said that they are asking for money.'

'Ahh, I think —!' He suddenly became stony-faced and looked as though he was about to lay bare his stratagems. I gazed at him with interest.

He didn't reveal a plan; he didn't say anything at all. Instead he broke into a fit of uproarious laughter.

'What is it?' I asked, feeling unsure.

Mani continued to laugh, so much so that tears began to well in his eyes. I couldn't help myself from joining in. It was too amusing to watch him, his eyes gleaming like a madman as he guffawed.

'What is it? Share the joke.'

Mani abruptly stopped, his tone serious but his face still grinning. 'Ah, it's okay, no problem for tourist.'

'No problem for tourist!' I wasn't convinced and he could see I was nervous.

'No problem, no problem,' he reiterated. 'Eat breakfast and have good time!' His tone became sterner, and he gestured at the table. Breakfast had arrived.

We both munched quietly on our food, although my appetite had faded. Now I ate out of necessity rather than desire. My spirits had been dampened a bit and the Tibetan bread tasted bland.

The words of an ex-girlfriend came into my mind: 'Smile like an eejit,' she said, 'even when you're pissed off. Eventually your brain gets the message to cheer itself up.' I forced my lips into a smile and, yes, moments later I felt much better. Maybe that was what Mani did, too.

Revived, we started off again. Within a hundred metres or so we came to the huge stone anchors of a rope bridge. Below it, a powerful, gushing river flowed. The bridge looked unsteady to me until I watched five cows thunder past us. Under the unwavering direction of their whipping master they crossed the chasm with Mani and me close behind. Moments later we were all safely on the other side.

Mani led the way to a cottage not far from the bridge. There was no sign on the door, but the small queue of fellow backpackers was sign enough that this was the trekking registration point of Birethanti. Inside was only one room, and apart from a few maps taped to the walls, there was just a large bound logbook on the centre of an unsteady wooden table. Since the room was not staffed, Mani pointed out what to do.

A couple of signatures later we were really on the trek. Mani seemed so enthusiastic that I felt it rubbing off on me. I recited a short prayer, and thankfully got it correct the first time. Thumbs pointing up, eyes looking to the sky, toes pointing in a vertical manner inside my boots as I teetered on my heels — what an ordeal! Still, I was pleased that my mind had obliged so agreeably.

I'm not actually a religious person — the whole praying concept was something I'd developed as a crutch to lean on when I was worried or bothered. But over time, the more I did it the more I'd come to rely on it and now, after twenty years, the prayers had become almost as necessary to me as breathing.

Doctors had told my parents that this was a form of OCD — Obsessive Compulsive Disorder. In the same way that there are people who can't leave their houses without turning the light switch off and on a hundred times, my praying placed similar mental demands on me. It was never a case of simply praying; it was much more than that; it was about perfection. Every syllable of every prayer had to be recited precisely and only at that point, when my mind was entirely satisfied that there were no errors, could I feel content enough to stop reciting. It sounds crazy and I suppose it is.

As our journey became decidedly uphill, Mani, showing his experience, powered off in front, leaving me straggling some distance behind. It was too early in the day to be lagging. I quickened my pace and was soon following closely at his heels. As I walked I thought about the registration in Birethanti.

Who would find you out here? The countryside was vast and secretive, a short stray from the trekking path would surely lead you, unsuspecting, into depths of forests that you'd struggle to resurface from. I shivered at the notion that the registration centre represented a final record: if you went missing, the only proof that you were ever here was your name in a book in Birethanti!

I wondered how many people got lost every year? What a stupid thought! I was angry that I was thinking this way. I'm not praying about this, you can forget it!

I managed to put these thoughts aside and concentrate instead on hauling my legs up the steep slope. The walking was intense, and maintaining a steady pace became more important than appreciating the surroundings. When I did stop for a breather, redirecting my eyes from their hypnotic focus on my feet, I found that we had walked for an hour and in that time the landscape had become much more open and farmland was dominating the view. We'd climbed at least a thousand metres.

3. Caterpillars and Dhanyabaad

My brother John was older than me by three years. Even as a child he was tall and sturdy for his age and it was no surprise that as soon as he hit high school he was a popular team member in most sports. Whatever he put his hand to he was a natural at. Along with his gift for the usual sports of soccer and athletics, John was adventurous — he also gave extreme sports a go: rock climbing, parachuting, bungee jumping; he did whatever came his way. He was very much my older and wiser brother and there never seemed to be anything too difficult or out of reach for him. When we were kids together, he would take me across railway tracks and down by old quarries; everything we did seemed, through my young eyes, to be dangerous but so exciting. He watched over me and inspired me at the same time.

John and I had drifted apart as we got older. Our lives had moved on from the common interests of childhood to solo paths. John was focused on his career and settling down with a partner, while I was, in my own way, still fancy free and trying to find myself. Holidays and trips abroad seemed a thing of the past for John. Nepal would have thrilled him, but I couldn't imagine him ever coming here. Too many chains were wrapped around him.

Mani stopped abruptly. We had walked up what felt like five hundred steps and he needed a break. So did I.

I hadn't expected it to be so hot. It wasn't quite midday yet but the sun was strong. The green cotton vest I wore had become uncomfortable and clung to me in a heavy coating of sweat. Patches of dense forest tempered the heat but so far they'd been in short supply. For the most part we'd trekked through unsheltered hillsides.

Don't start moaning, I told myself. Enjoy being here. Nepal is like a dream. Each time I told that to myself, it gave me a jolt of energy. I was out of breath, thirsty and sticky all over, but all in all, at that early stage of the trek, I was pretty good. A long journey still lay ahead, but my legs were feeling strong.

'Where you come from?' asked Mani, sitting himself on a fallen tree trunk as I gulped water from my canister.

'Ireland,' I replied.

'Holland?'

'No, *Ireland*.' After so many years living abroad, I didn't sound Irish any more than I sounded English.

'Ah, island,' he deciphered. Despite his pronunciation being incorrect, I could see he'd understood. He looked away thoughtfully, the backpack released from his sturdy shoulders. He seemed relaxed but distant.

'Would you like some water?' I held the flask in front of him.

'Ah.' He thought for a moment. 'No, *dhanyabaad*.'

'Danye?' I couldn't pronounce it. 'What's that?'

'Ah, it means thank you. *Dhanyabaad* — thank you.'

'Oh.' I repeated it. '*Dhanyabaad*.'

'Yes, *dhanyabaad*, thank you, very good.' He was pleased and glowed like a proud teacher.

I repeated it a few more times to myself. *Dhanyabaad, dhanyabaad*, DAN — YOU — BAT. I never really liked cricket, but picturing some unknown friend Dan being pushed up to bat seemed to be the best way of remembering the word. Better than visualising it, which was the other way I usually memorised things. I have always tried to make a point of remembering as many details that come my way as possible; names in particular.

Dhanyabaad. It was firm in my mind.

'Okay, we go.' Mani secured the backpack to his shoulders and, with a heavy sigh, lifted himself to his feet. I watched as the veins protruded from his short legs. How strong was this little man?

Mani didn't have one ounce of fat on his body. He was almost all muscle, like an extremely athletic boy. His physique, I thought now, could have only been achieved through years of hard graft and many a day without sweets and delicacies. Now, as I watched him leaning forward, controlling the weight of my bag while at the same time tackling the steep incline, I couldn't imagine how he felt, though I knew he'd done the trip countless times before and must have been used to weights far heavier than mine.

Dear Holy God, please protect Mam and Dad, John, Sarah and Sam, Benji and Rusty, all my friends and relatives and everybody who needs your help today. I paused. *And Mani with the backpack.*

That was a bad sign. It was only my first day and already my mind was introducing new additions to the ritual. I had promised myself before I arrived in Nepal that I was going to battle this sickness, make a huge effort not to pray, or, for that matter, not to worry. Already I was departing from the plan!

And Mani with the backpack! What an idiot. I was disappointed with myself.

No doubt Mani knew every aspect of trekking like the back of his hand. What could my few words possibly do to help him? He seemed capable and he'd survived well enough up until that point without my assistance.

Mani doesn't need to be in my prayer, I thought, and I don't need him there either. I've enough problems of my own without worrying about his! He's just another name to torment me.

As my irritation increased I felt a sudden urge to recite the prayer again. I pointed my eyes, fingers and toes to the sky and hoped for no interruptions which would require me to start again. It was awkward and uncomfortable walking on my heels like this — a ridiculous position for trekking.

It's just typical! You can't cure everybody else's problems, you're a fool if you think that you can. We're all masters of our own destiny! I'm not including him —

Dear Holy God, please protect Mam and Dad, John, Sarah and Sam, Benji and Rusty, all my friends and relatives and everybody who needs your help today.

The words melted away as we neared a small village and I was obliged to greet some travellers heading in the opposite direction.

'*Namaste*!' I said cheerfully. Now I had to silently repeat the prayer again. *Dear Holy God, please protect Mam and Dad, John, Sarah and Sam, Benji and Rusty, all my friends and relatives and everybody who needs your help today and Mani with the backpack.*

It was perfect but it left an ill taste in my mouth. I shouldn't have been so weak.

'Alright, mate.' He was British and was in front of his porter and his guide. All three appeared to be in a hurry.

'Where have you just come from?' I asked.

'Came straight from Ghorepani today. Bloody Maoists are everywhere up there!'

'Really, are you serious?'

'Bloody right, mate. I'm not hanging around in these mountains. It's just a matter of time before the little bastards start taking tourists as hostages.'

His voice was full of scorn, and while I didn't doubt there were Maoists up ahead I remembered my dad's words again: 'Always look like you're prepared when you're travelling — people are more accepting of you when they think you're one of their own.'

The Briton was dressed entirely in expensive North Face hiking gear, which looked brand-new. He must have bought it all just before he left England. An oversized Nikon ultra-zoom camera dangled ostentatiously around his neck, and printed on his hat was the slogan 'I conquered the Annapurna'. His bum bag was bulging.

Dad was right. My own most frightening moments when I started travelling had all been when I looked out of place or acted like I was better than other people.

'I was a sitting duck if I stayed,' the guy continued.

'Did you have to pay them anything?' I asked, trying to bat away his fear from me.

'Nah, I didn't stay long enough. No one's getting a penny out of me, I'm telling you!' He wiped sweat from his forehead, his skin blotchy red under the heat. 'Hey, if I were you I wouldn't go up there. It's a death trap!' His voice was intense and for a minute I was swayed by it. Mani broke the spell.

'I think we better go, keep moving! Maoist no problem!'

The British guy was appalled.

'Maoist no problem? Have you got bleeding cement between your ears? They're a big bloody problem. They're going to put you boys out of work, for one thing!'

He was speaking fast and I could tell from the glazed look in Mani's eyes that he didn't understand everything the bloke was saying.

'Do you think tourists are going to bother coming up here if their lives are at risk? No bloody way! When I get back to England I'll be telling my government all about this, and believe me, nobody will be coming here then, mate!'

Mani interrupted this speech abruptly, turning away as he spoke. 'We better go, no problem!'

The British traveller didn't hide his disapproval and I saw a certain anger creep in. Mani was disregarding him and he wasn't impressed. I followed Mani.

'Suit yourselves, mates, but don't expect me to be part of your search party when you go missing!' He was terribly rattled.

Stealing a quick glance back, I watched as he bad-temperedly nudged past both his guide and porter and sped down the hill, then finally disappeared around a bend. Mani, on the other hand, had begun singing softly to himself. At first I thought it was a smug song of victory but on nearing him I realised that he was quite contentedly singing for the simple pleasure of a tune. It was contagious. Before long, I found myself humming a song as well. Music had been my lifeline for years back in Ireland. When I sang and played, my spirits lifted and I felt open to the good life had to offer.

The path ahead was still very exposed, with little shelter from the scorching sun, but the views were enthralling. Expanses of green stretching high into the clouds, clinging tightly to white water washing over falls and becoming frantically flowing rivers below. It was painterly but there was also a realness to the countryside that was quite unlike anything I'd seen before. Nothing was fabricated, nothing was false; it was all natural and engaging. A part of me wished for little more than to stop what I was doing, find a patch of grass to sit upon, and simply close my eyes and listen. There was so much of nature on display and I could not give it my full attention.

We continued at a steady pace for about four miles until at last we found ourselves walking beneath a patch of trees. Up ahead a large number of children in school uniforms were coming towards us, and to clear the path for them we took a break. I swigged from my water canister and greeted the children as they passed. Mani offloaded my backpack from his shoulders and I was amazed to see steam emanating from its surface.

'They go to school in Birethanti!' Mani must have been reading my mind.

'All the way to Birethanti?' I gasped, a little higher pitched than I intended.

'Yes.' He started to giggle. 'Long walk!' His giggle developed into convulsions of laughter, just like earlier and I suddenly felt like the shy kid who never caught the dirty joke at school but laughed anyway.

Yet how amazing it was that these children made such a trip to school, and wearing only a pair of flip-flops. There I stood in my heavy boots and all my hiking clothes, while they skipped by in school uniforms and next to nothing on their feet, calling '*Namaste*,' their eyes glowing in their fresh handsome faces.

Mam's words resounded in my head. 'Which shoes do you want?' she had quizzed, as the shop assistant stood waiting.

'I don't like either pair. They both look so nerdy!' I'd replied indignantly.

'They're just school shoes, it doesn't matter what they look like!'

Protesting with Mam was pointless. Once her mind was made up, there was no changing it.

'And tomorrow you can walk to school. It'll do you the world of good!' she went on.

'Ah, but, Mam, it'll take me ages.'

My primary school was probably less than five minutes from our house, but in the end I only ever walked the distance, at most, four or five times.

Mani grabbed hold of my arm, startling me slightly.

'Look!' He stretched out an arm and pointed to the surrounding foliage. 'Can you see?'

I looked intently, trying hard to follow where he was pointing but saw nothing. 'No. What is it?'

'*Look*,' he said again, this time pointing more definitely.

I squinted my eyes but still saw nothing. 'I still can't see anything. What is it?'

Mani bent down and picked up a stone. 'Look now,' he said as he threw it.

The stone was a direct hit and a giant caterpillar tumbled from a leaf and fell out of view. Mani laughed again.

'Ah, a caterpillar,' I said, amused by Mani's stoning of it. 'A dead caterpillar,' I laughed. 'It was very big, maybe the size of my hand.'

'Caterplow ...' Mani didn't recognise the word.

'No, *caterpillar*.'

'Cater ... caiterplo ... Ah yes, butterfly!'

Was he joking? 'Yes, kind of!' A moment of silence followed.

'I become married next year, you know?'

'You're getting married?' I looked at him. 'Oh, nice one. What's your girlfriend's name?'

'Ah, Mani have no girl but now I am thirty-eight which is very old for Nepali man. Next year I must marry or Mani have no chance!' Mani's face lit up as he spoke and it was clear that the prospect of marriage excited him greatly.

'You have no girl but you are getting married? How?'

Mani stared at me briefly then turned away and slyly laughed to himself. After a few moments he returned his gaze to me, this time with renewed seriousness.

'Ah, right now I have plan! Before, I think maybe I was unlucky?'

Mani let this last line hang and threw me a

questioning look, as though he wished me to confirm his bad luck. I couldn't, so he continued.

'Yes, maybe, I think, I have bad luck. Now Mani has plan though — no drinking, no ganja, only *dal bhat*. Only *dal bhat* for me and I am saving my money!'

I began to understand the direction of the conversation.

'You have arranged marriages in Nepal?' I asked, but Mani looked at me blankly. 'When you are getting married, do you know your wife for a long time before the wedding or do you meet for the first time on the wedding day?'

'Ah marriage, I understand,' he replied with excitement. 'If I work hard, the mothers they see. They see if I am good man, if I work hard, if I drink not so much and no ganja. Now I eat only *dal bhat*. The mothers they see that I am saving and that I am good, but still I need build house and then mothers give me daughter.'

'So have you picked a daughter that you like?'

Mani's eyes opened wide with delight and an embarrassed kind of happiness.

'I see one girl —' he broke off into bashful laughter.

'Is she the same age as you?' But I knew she wouldn't be. Almost every married Nepalese man I'd seen seemed to have a wife almost half his age by his side.

'No,' he replied. 'I am old, thirty-eight, I tell you very old for Nepali man. She is younger, maybe twenty-two!' Again his face lit up with a smile. 'Maybe nineteen.'

'Nineteen!' I said, playing along with him. 'Oh, that's very young. So young for somebody so much older!' Mani seemed quite taken with the idea.

'In Nepal many wives younger than man. I have to work hard, make much money, build house. If I do, I catch mother's eyes, if she happy, then I can marry daughter. But it takes long time and all woman married before twenty-five years — so I only get young girl.'

'So you have to prove yourself!'

'Yes. If I am doing well, no drinking, then I get better type wife!'

I chuckled. 'A better quality wife?'

Mani found it amusing as well. 'Yes, a better type wife. If I am working bad, save no money, I get no wife or wife not so good kind.'

We both looked off into the distance and contented ourselves with our separate thoughts. I felt guilty to be thinking it, but I now wondered if Mani was a virgin. He must be!

A few minutes passed and then almost instinctively we rose at the same time to begin trekking again.

Mani set off well ahead of me and led the way out from the comfort of our shelter, back into the blistering heat. My feet were starting to feel the pinch of this forever-uphill trail, and I tried to distract myself by thinking of other things.

Why, at thirty-eight, hadn't Mani been married yet? His references to not drinking or smoking weed as his main challenge in winning a young lady — or her mother — had seemed overdone. Isn't that what all mothers want? Observing Mani, he didn't strike me as somebody who had skeletons in his cupboard but perhaps I was wrong. It made me question if there was more to Mani's 'bad luck' than just being unfortunate. Bad luck was not something that I believed in now; over time I had convinced myself it didn't exist. When I was younger though, rather than do anything about my ritual praying, I'd thought, if I could only have a stroke of luck then I'd wake up one day and the damn praying would have gone away. But I'm not lucky!

It all began when I was about six. Very young. I started not sleeping at night. I couldn't seem to switch my mind off. I used to lie in the dark visualising terrifying images in the shadows. I wouldn't intentionally try to scare myself; at first I would be trying to picture Santa Claus or Mickey Mouse — happy things that would help me relax. Gradually, though, the images would change and before I knew it, Santa would be wielding a sharp knife and Mickey would have transformed into the devil. It scared the life out of me. But as soon as I'd snuck into bed beside my little sister, Sarah, or youngest brother, Sam, the images would disappear and I would be asleep in seconds. Their rooms had the same shadows, the same darkness — that didn't matter as long as I was in beside somebody else.

At the beginning my parents must have thought I would soon grow out of it. Why wouldn't they think that? Many kids are frightened to sleep on their own. But at age thirteen I was still creeping in beside Sarah or Sam. It was embarrassing. I was older than both of them for Godsake. How weird was it to be sleeping with your brother or sister at thirteen? It was like still wetting your bed.

Then, almost overnight, I suddenly became obsessed with germs. I started washing my hands in a strange way; repeatedly and methodically for hours at a time. I had to be convinced that all possible germs had been removed. It was insane — but there was nothing I could do about it. And it worsened. Every time I had to wash my hands it was as though a brick wall formed inside my mind and the only way I could break it down was to precisely and correctly perform the washing. The frustration was unbearable and I was always stressed and agitated.

Then shortly after I'd started the hand-washing ritual I developed another ritual involving my feet. A sensation would come over my foot which required me to rub the other foot over it until this sensation was gone. There was nothing physical about this sensation — it was entirely in my head. I knew this, but the ritual burrowed in to become a driving force. As I wore out shoe after shoe, my parents were forever asking why.

I knew the solution was simple: stop doing it. But stopping was a much greater task than it sounded. Then again I didn't care about my shoes. I could get new ones. But what about my hands?

Excessive hand-washing took its toll and it wasn't long before my hands became dry and worn. Cuts and cracks soon followed.

'Mammy, Sean has something wrong with his hands! Mammy go look, go look!'

Sarah and I had been playing with each other and the fun had turned into an argument. She pinched me, then I pinched her back. She slapped me and I returned the slap. The coarseness of my hands shocked Sarah.

'What did you hit me with? What have you got in there?' She wailed and grabbed my hands to see what they were hiding.

I whipped them away. I'd washed them for over an hour that morning, and they were in a terrible state by afternoon.

'Sean, show me your hands,' my mam demanded. Reluctantly I opened them up and let her look.

'Sean, what have you been doing to yourself?' she exclaimed, examining my broken skin.

'Nothing, nothing!' I retorted with embarrassment. I tried to pull my hands back from her but she dragged me closer.

'Your hands are in bits. Did you hurt yourself?'

'*No!*'

Mam regarded me sternly; she knew that I wasn't lying but I was obviously not telling her the facts either.

'We'll show them to your father!'

I was petrified.

Mam didn't show my hands to Dad, and looking back on those days I think that it must have dawned on her then that there was more to my problems than just adolescence. She took to watching me like a hawk.

I don't look back on those years with fondness. Life was a terrible struggle for me. Every day was spent trying desperately to hide my problems. And I was good at hiding them. I would wait until no one was in the house to do the hand-washing, and all my other rituals I did when backs were turned or people were distracted.

The turning point was one morning at around one o'clock when my sister said, 'Not tonight, not any more. You're too old to be sleeping with anyone. You're like a baby. What's wrong with you anyway?'

'Ah, just tonight, just one more night. I can't sleep alone. I'm frightened.'

I sounded like an addict, only concerned about one thing — my needs. Intent, focused, I was oblivious to what my sister had said to me.

'No, get out. You're too old, get out!'

Sarah had talked like this before that night, but never with such determination.

'Ah, come on, Sars, please. I'm serious — I really can't sleep. I promise I'll sleep on my own tomorrow night. Please just tonight. This will be the last time.'

Jumping out of bed, Sarah powered towards me and grabbed me by the arm.

'Out!' she exclaimed in fury, as she led me from the

room and into the hallway. 'You have to sleep on your own from now on, Sean.'

'But, Sarah, I can't. I just can't! I'm scared!'

'I don't care,' she replied rigidly. 'Sam has locked his bedroom door and so will I. You're on your own. No more of this!'

'Please,' I begged in a whisper, worried that Mam and Dad would wake up with all the commotion.

'No, Sean. You're being pathetic and if you keep doing this —' she hesitated — 'I'm going to end up hating you!'

Sarah's eyes were filled with such resolution I had nothing more to say. What could I say? Seconds later she was gone and I heard her bedroom door locking. Suddenly I was alone; it was just the darkness and me. At first I considered turning the hall lights on, but decided not to — I had to be brave.

I had nowhere to go, Sam and Sarah had locked me out and John was out of the question. I couldn't possibly have gone to Mam and Dad. I realised for the first time that night, as I stood barefooted on the cold hallway floor, just how foolish I was. A thirteen-year-old who slept with his brother or sister every night — if anyone heard about it they would have laughed their heads off. People might have even thought it was perverse, which was the furthest thing from the truth.

It wasn't just a case of being utterly frightened of sleeping alone: it was the fear of closing my eyes and not knowing what was happening in the room from then on. That's what bothered me most: the fear of not knowing. Having somebody beside me relieved that fear enough to feel safe and to sleep soundly.

I sat down on the floor with my knees tucked up close to my chin. I began to feel sorry for myself, mainly because I felt stupid.

The night stretched on endlessly. I was exhausted but just too frightened to close my eyes. Each time I felt myself nodding off I would wake with a fright.

What's there?

There was nothing there; it was still just me and the hallway.

You're an absolute chicken!

I don't know when it happened but sometime in the dark of that night I drifted off to sleep. I woke up lying in the same position on the hallway floor, astonished I had made it through the night. The sunlight that crept through the hallway curtains was the brightest and most comforting I'd ever seen. I couldn't believe I'd managed on my own. It was still very early morning but I was ecstatic.

Tired but triumphant, I climbed into my own bed, and within minutes I went back to sleep. That night had been a breakthrough. When I awoke there was a note at the foot of my bed. '*Well done, Sean, so proud of you. Love Sarah.*' I still have that note.

And just like that, I was sleeping on my own every night. I stopped my hand-washing ritual. I even managed to cut back on the foot-rubbing too. It felt as though a weight had been lifted, a weight I'd been carrying for too long. Shortly afterwards the praying began.

4. *Three thousand steps*

'Okay, we eat here, lunch.'

We had reached a small village, about three hours from our intended destination of Ulleri. The village was simple, not more than three guesthouses and a number of small barns. Apart from the blue roofs on the buildings, it blended chameleon-like with the surrounding countryside, the buildings overgrown with plants and trees and the brickwork weathered brown, so that you barely noticed the village until you were almost upon it. A group of young children scurried out as we arrived. They greeted us with such cheer it was as though we were arriving home.

Mani pointed to one of the huts.

'We eat there.'

I was starved and would have eaten anywhere.

A middle-aged Nepalese man emerged from the teahouse. He had a gentle face and a welcome grin which he directed towards Mani — they were obviously friends — and immediately began to converse in Nepali. Suddenly I felt like a spare tyre. Mani would be more comfortable eating here with his friend, especially since quite likely he'd order *dal bhat*.

Eaten with the bare left hand, *dal bhat* was quite messy. The idea of the dish was simple: add lentils to rice, eat it with the spicy onions and follow that with a hefty portion of the potatoes — generously washed down with plain yogurt. I had tried it on many occasions in India and found it to be quite pasty and tasteless. Years of growing up eating stews and lentil soups had killed off my palate for such dishes.

'*Dal bhat* at eleven in the morning,' Mani had explained, 'and again at four in the afternoon. Then at the night, seven o'clock and maybe again before sleeping.'

'That's a lot of *dal bhat*.'

'Mani love,' he had replied, rubbing his stomach for effect.

So much of the same food, I thought, couldn't be healthy, let alone interesting. It was economical alright, and easy to make in bulk. But still, I didn't like the taste of it. I chose something different at this teahouse — noodle soup and a bottle of Coca-Cola and retired to the company of my own thoughts. Mani opted to eat lunch with his friend and I found myself alone.

'What's wrong?'

At seventeen I was shocked to see Mam crying. She was alone, the living room was cold and the television hummed quietly in the background. Mam gave me a sorrowful smile.

'Nothing,' she finally replied. 'Nothing to worry you. You go on off and do whatever you have to do!'

Mam was an upright woman with a heart of gold. Her protective sternness had never bothered me; though she was strict she was also the most loving mother any child could ever hope for. If we were punished it was because we genuinely deserved it and most times it was simply a scolding.

I sat down and put my arm around her. She needed a hug. 'What are you thinking about? Tell me!'

Mam was also a very proud woman, and this was one of the first times that I'd seen her defences lowered. I could tell she wasn't too comfortable with me trying to help. But eventually she spoke.

'You're all getting older!' she finally whispered. Tears began again and I embraced her tighter.

There were many things I wanted to say, but I had no words that would ease her mind. We *were* all growing up and it frightened her deeply; it frightened me too. Mam had devoted her life to us and suddenly, before her eyes, we were slowly drifting away, relying on other people and other things.

A prayer was forming in my mind. Mani suddenly appeared and caught me unawares.

'You not eat!'

I looked down at my food. I'd hardly eaten anything, even though I was so hungry. But now I needed to concentrate on the words of the prayer that ran through my head! What must he have thought of me as I stared past him in a bit of daze?

The prayer went well and I felt content that Mam would be okay.

'I'll eat it now,' I finally replied. To Mani's surprise, I began to scoff down my food.

Are they pissed off with me, I wondered as I ate. What must Mam and Dad — and John — think? Since I'd been in Nepal I'd resisted brooding on what state my family would be in and I was alarmed that the idea should come to me now. Yes, I'd fled Ireland. It was the wrong thing to do, but what was done was done. I finished the remainder of my lunch. 'Alright, how far to Ulleri?' I was being too enthusiastic now.

Mani raised an arm and pointed towards the forested mountain that towered over this small village.

'Oh, no! You've got to be joking.' But Mani wasn't joking.

'You see —' he pointed towards a tiny blue dot high in the distance. A building, barely visible, nestled deep within the forest at the top of the mountain. I'd noticed most houses along the trek had blue corrugated rooftops.

'That is our next teahouse — we rest there tonight.'

'Ah, Christ almighty,' I moaned. It had to be at least a thousand metres, and practically vertical! 'That's going to take forever!'

'Three thousand steps,' Mani replied. 'Maybe three hours' walking.'

Mani's friend from the teahouse overheard our conversation. 'Maybe you would like to stay in my hotel tonight instead and start fresh tomorrow morning?'

'Ah, no, maybe next time.' I knew this was the best response to make. 'I would rather get it over and done with today.'

Mani threw an approving glance in my direction; it felt good.

'You sure? Nice rooms, very cheap!' the manager persisted.

'Thank you, but no, we better go.'

The manager blurted something to Mani in Nepali and both men gave a cautious laugh. Had he commented how fit and courageous I was, not to give in for the night at such an early stage of the trek? No, more likely he just said I was a tight wanker.

Mani once again set off purposefully, over a wooden bridge, across a gentle clear stream and finally to step number one of our three thousand! Before we'd reached the first rocky slab of the staircase I'd decided that, no matter what came or went, I wouldn't count them. But — *one, two, three, four* — it was like counting sheep except the pain in the legs reminded you that, yes, you were still awake and, no, you hadn't reached the top yet … 299, 300, 301, 302. It was so goddamn steep! I glanced back at the height we had already travelled.

If somebody fell here it would be one heck of a drop!

I didn't like that thought; once again it made me think of my family. *You're worrying too much. They're all fine.* I calculated that it would be about seven in the morning back in Ireland. Dad would probably be driving off to work.

Dad always used to ring me on my mobile in the mornings on his way to work. He never talked about much, just wanted to make contact. Dad, like Mam, lived for us kids. What if he collided with a truck en route? What if his tyre had a blow-out?

I tried to banish these thoughts with a short prayer, but I couldn't complete it — each step of our ascent needed my concentration. Yet the anxiety of the prayer weighed heavier and heavier. And because of the prayer's incompleteness it was only a matter of time before I'd have more thoughts of home and terrible possibilities.

... 1003, 1004, 1005, 1006 ...

Unfinished prayers led to guilt and fear. Now I was fearful that because I didn't complete the prayer Dad *would* have an accident. It would be through no fault of his, it would be because of my unfinished prayer. I began silently reciting the prayer again — but it was too difficult and I couldn't get it right. Each new step met me faster than the time I needed to complete the prayer, and excluding stopping altogether and making it obvious to Mani that there was something wrong, there was nothing I could do.

But Mani had stopped up ahead. Before I reached him he had already taken the backpack off and was walking swiftly back towards me.

'You alright?' I asked, alarmed.

'I need piss!' he replied as he hurried by me and disappeared into a heavy patch of trees. His urgency was bizarre.

Ah, what a relief! There was nobody around, I was totally free of interruptions. With my eyes focused on the highest point in the sky and fingers and toes flexed, I finally had success.

'There's a lot going on in your head, Sean, isn't there?'

We lay beside each other. The beach hut was grey and bare but neither of us was much concerned with the surroundings. We were in India but we could have been anywhere in the world and we would have been oblivious to it. I was focused on her eyes and she on mine, that was all that mattered.

'What makes you think that?'

Her directness was a surprise; no one outside family had ever really commented before.

'You can tell,' she replied softly. 'Sometimes I talk to you and you're someplace else.'

She couldn't have been more on the money. I wanted to change the conversation, but I didn't know how.

'You don't need to say anything,' she continued. 'It doesn't matter to me.' Her face was lit up, her eyes glowing in the half light of our room. 'All you've got to do is keep those things under control. Don't let them take over your beautiful soul.' She wagged a playful finger at me. She instinctively knew more about me than most people I'd known for years. I felt comfortable that I didn't have to talk.

My mind was clear. I was sitting on the stone steps enjoying the scenery when Mani returned. He'd managed to sneak into my prayer again but now I didn't care. It was easier to add him than contend with the guilt of not adding him.

Mani sat down beside me — we were both exhausted, and the steps still stretched above us.

'Are we nearly halfway?' I asked optimistically.

'I think maybe ...' He paused to look up in the direction we were heading. 'Maybe no.'

'No!' It was a desperate *no*. I sighed. 'How far then?'

'Maybe still many steps, I think two more hours.'

Two more hours. It was a feat of science, never before had such scrawny legs achieved so much in such a short time.

At two-thirds of the way I was still counting the steps ... 2121, 2122, 2123, 2124 ... Was I intentionally trying to punish myself? I might as well have been counting each second it was taking. It was as painful as the trip to India from Ireland: nine-hours on a beautiful, shiny new Boeing 747, with all the trimmings, all the extras — including the option of viewing the journey on my own personal on-screen flight map showing miles to destination, time to destination, miles travelled since departing — it was a neurotic's nightmare, *14236 miles, 14225 miles, 14218 miles ...*

Mani sat down on one of the steps up ahead. He left the backpack on. As soon as I caught up I sat also and drank the remainder of my water.

'I think it's going to rain.' I indicated the gradual swoop of black clouds in our direction. At lunchtime I'd observed how far away they were and thought we would probably avoid them. Since then the wind must have shifted, and sometime during the hours between steps one thousand and two thousand we had begun climbing towards the clouds rather than away.

'I think not.' Mani gazed into the sky. 'I think today we will get lucky.' As he spoke I noticed for the first time that he'd begun to look tired and was breathing more heavily.

'Are you tired?'

'Ah, a little, not so bad.' Mani's face creased into a smile. 'Today, Mani not so fit, tomorrow and the next day, very fit!' He slapped his thighs for effect.

'Ah, good on you,' I laughed. 'At least one of us will be.'

'This season you are Mani's customer number one. I arrive from Kathmandu to Pokhara three weeks ago but no work until now, very bad time, I think — tourists not come to Nepal. Very bad time!'

'Yes, it is a very bad time,' I agreed. 'When I first arrived in Nepal, I didn't know as much about all of the fighting — if I had, I probably wouldn't have come.'

Not surprisingly, these words didn't cheer Mani up. You think that by agreeing with somebody you'll make them feel better, but you're actually rubbing salt into the wound. I went silent. There was an awkward pause and I threw a stone at a nearby tree. I missed.

'I do this job for fifteen years,' Mani began, sounding optimistic again. 'When I start we have many tourists and many work. It was good time but Mani not so interested in keeping money. Now I have plan for money and wife, but now no tourists. I think maybe I am unlucky — but I am happy because now I am not drinking and no ganja.'

'Did you drink a lot?'

It was an odd question, but I felt that Mani had led me there.

He smiled. 'Drink and Mani very good friends.' The conversation ended there, and that seemed like a good place to leave it. This was none of my business.

We started off again on what would be our last stretch of the day. Every bend, every hopeful ending met once again with a vertical staircase. Secretly I had hoped that Mani had been mistaken when he'd said it was three thousand steps. In fact, he had underestimated. At the three-thousand-steps mark, Ulleri finally came into view, but we were at least ten minutes' walk away.

When at last we hobbled into the quiet streets of the town, I was shattered by the marathon.

Ulleri was a small village quite similar to Birethanti. Mani chose a guesthouse from the six available and negotiated a fair price. I crawled up the final insult of the day, a staircase to the bedrooms, and plonked my aching body down onto the hard surface of my bed. Relief!

But Mani must have read my mind. He knocked on the door.

'The shower has hot water. I think that you should wash!'

Did I smell that bad?

'You want *dal bhat* tonight?' Mani's tone suggested that *dal bhat* was probably the best choice for the night, so I agreed, then made my way to the shower.

This was a small guesthouse, scantily decorated and with cold wooden floorboards throughout. A rough but pleasant place for weary bodies.

The shower was in an outhouse next to a smelly squat toilet — a hole in the ground over which you hovered to do your business. Standing under the shower, I watched the lukewarm water fall from my body and form a puddle at my feet. The size of the puddle increased. Alarmingly, it soon reached the perimeter of the toilet — eventually flowing into it.

I looked down at the puddle. What's a bit of piss on your feet?

Grimacing, I dried myself off and got dressed. I was content to have day one over and to be out of my trekking gear and into something more comfortable, particularly the flip-flops on my aching feet.

* * *

'Ah, my name is, eh, Akio.' He was sitting alone at one of the wooden tables when I entered, but quickly rose to greet me. Another tourist!

'Akio,' I tried. 'Nice to meet you. My name is Sean.'

'Sean, good-o.' He pulled a small notebook from his pocket and began to scribble in it. 'I write your name so I not-o forget.'

I smiled, it was hard not to.

The room seemed like a greenhouse, though it was the restaurant. We sat down.

'Where are you from?' I asked him.

'I come on bus to Nayapul and I trek to Ulleri from there!'

I had to smile again. 'No — which country do you come from? I'm from Ireland.'

'Oh, I see,' he exclaimed enthusiastically. 'I am residence of Japan.'

'Japan? Very good,' I said cheerfully. 'And have you been in Nepal for long?'

'I stay for two weeks only. You?'

'Oh, I don't know. I'm travelling until I get tired of it all.' He looked at me confused, so I decided to clarify. 'Until my money runs out.'

He understood and gave an acknowledging nod. He was a short man, in his early twenties, of a sturdy, hefty build. His face was youthful and unlined and his stance expressed an enthusiastic confidence, which was refreshing.

'So, how far are you trekking?' I asked.

'Not so far, I only go to Tadapani. I want to see hot-o springs.'

'Hot springs?' I replied. 'I didn't know there were hot springs in Tadapani.'

'Yes. *Tada*, it mean hot; *pani*, it mean water. You go to Tadapani also?'

'No, I'm going to Annapurna Base camp, in a different direction.'

I knew the route he was taking; we'd both be travelling to Ghorepani but then we would go our separate ways. His way would see him to the hot springs and back to Pokhara in four days; mine would take eight or nine. Feeling the pain in my legs, I was slightly envious of him.

'So do you travel alone? Have you no porter?'

Akio seemed confused by my question. 'I have good map. He is my guide!'

Mani broke up the conversation as he entered the room; he was showered and looking very fit. With him he brought a friendly black dog, which paraded around the room seeking attention.

Mani had already met with Akio while I showered. They began trying to impress one another with how much of each other's language they knew. I was content to pet the dog and be reminded of my own two dogs, Benji and Rusty. They were like two extra kids in the house. Benji had never developed the quick assertiveness of his mother, Rusty. He'd grown to be a huge bear of a dog, utterly harmless in every way and never smart enough to be trained to do anything other than eat, drink and roll over for a rub.

'Leechee, leechee!' The yell came from Akio first, then both men sprang into action. There was a big leech on the dog's head!

Stuck tight to the dog's right ear was a fat leech about six centimetres in length, filled from the day's feeding. And I hadn't noticed a thing! It was the first leech I had ever seen, and it was disgusting. Akio promptly pulled a box of matches from his pocket. Quickly he began to strike a match along the side of the box but with no success. The matches were made from candle wax and weren't very strong — each strike broke the stick in the middle and Akio was forced to try another and another. Mani approached the situation more calmly. Lifting the shaker from the table, he slowly poured salt onto the leech. Within seconds the leech began to shrivel up, and finally its grip on the dog failed and it fell to the floor, wriggling helplessly. Mani's flip-flopped foot came down hard and fast on the leech; it took three crashing blows before the leech finally gave in.

'Oh leechee, very bad,' Akio was excited. 'My matches no good-o. I tried to burn but no good-o.'

'I didn't even see the damn thing,' I said, still surprised by the whole affair.

The dog wasn't fazed by its ordeal and in fact was now enjoying Mani's attentions.

'Tomorrow I think we will see leechees.' Mani spoke thoughtfully. 'Rain coming tonight, bringing many leechees tomorrow!'

Shit.

'What's tomorrow like? Have we got many steps again?' It seemed like a good idea to know what lay ahead.

Akio answered. 'Tomorrow has jungle, not as difficult as today — am I right?' He looked at Mani.

'Tomorrow not difficult, today very difficult. I think too difficult for first day.' Mani shooed the dog away and stretched his legs.

Then the *dal bhat* arrived. Serving up our meal was a young Nepalese girl, perhaps in her late teens, maybe even early twenties. She had slightly slanted eyes, fair skin, well-defined cheekbones and a small, well-suited nose and mouth. She was slim and when she entered the room all three of us became silent and attentive. I thought she was very beautiful.

A year earlier when I'd ended a three-year relationship, my brother John had said, consolingly, 'You'll get over it.'

'I'm already over it,' I'd replied. 'We were finished months ago. We just hung in there for routine.'

'Then what's wrong with you? You look upset.'

'Nothing. It's got me thinking.'

John was only half interested. 'What?'

'Relationships are about so much more than good looks. Next girlfriend I find will be somebody whose personality I hit it off with straightaway. If she's good looking as well, that'll just be a bonus.'

The Nepalese girl delicately served Mani and me a large helping each of *dal bhat*, while Akio tucked in to his choice of Tibetan bread, custard and fried potatoes. We ate in silence, too fatigued to talk, each of us lost in our own thoughts.

I watched as the Nepalese girl left our company and

imagined the life she was leading in Ulleri. Back home a girl like her would have her choice of men and, at this age, would be experiencing life at its most exciting. In Nepal she was one of so many confined to a hard life, which would include a husband and a tribe of children. It seemed so young to be so old.

My own parents, who'd married young, would say that hard times lead to hard measures, people grow up faster when they know they have to. I pondered it … if a child of nine has to hold down a badly paid job so that their contribution ensures that the whole family has a place to sleep at night, well, surely with that must come early insight into adulthood? I supposed that was where Nepal was sitting in the bigger scheme of things: a poor country excluded from the advancement of the rest of the world, progressing with whatever tools it had to survive. It was sad.

Akio suddenly broke my train of thought. 'I hear there are many bandits in Ghorepani, is it true?'

Bandits — that was a word I hadn't heard in a while. Mani hadn't understood, so I answered.

'The Maoists, yes, I heard that they are in Ghorepani and they look for donations from tourists.'

'Oh!' Akio seemed unimpressed. 'Oh, very bad.' Silence fell again in the room.

'I travel with you tomorrow,' Akio started again. 'I now travel alone, but maybe safer from bandits if we all travel together.'

It was strange and comical watching Akio, the nuts and bolts in his head intelligently and methodically figuring the way through a problem. While he thought out the difficulty, his face made many contortions.

'Hey, the more the merrier.' Despite feeling the odd sense of danger when they were mentioned, I was still not overly concerned about the Maoists. They remained in the shadows of my other consuming anxieties. 'What time tomorrow, Mani?'

Mani smiled at me, knowing I wouldn't be pleased. 'I think we leave at six o'clock and maybe breakfast at five-thirty.'

A long day tomorrow! I decided to call it a night. When I reached my room it was five past eight, but I was wrecked. The room was freezing at this high altitude, but at the end of the day, a bed is a bed.

I lay in the dark trying to recite my final prayers of the evening. Nine-thirty came and went. Almost an hour and thirty minutes of exhausted praying, before I fell asleep.

5. Spasms

Excruciating pain pierced my sleep. I lunged at my right leg like a security guard at a thief.

Even in the dim light of the room, I could see the extent of the spasm. I groaned. My entire calf muscle had contracted so tightly that the muscle looked like something growing out of my leg. In a half-awake panic I began rubbing the cramp with the palms of my hands, just to heat the muscle, to release its painful grasp on me. But this was useless.

Breathe, Sean, just breathe. Come on, just relax.

More awake now, I started to remember. I released my palms from the leg and began trying to quieten down.

I'd had many muscle spasms when I was a kid. From being one of the shortest in school, I'd grown late and fast into an average-sized young man. Suddenly I was getting almost nightly attacks of cramp, in either leg. Instinctively I'd tried to rub the muscles, to push them back into place.

'Stop shouting like that,' my brother John yelled one night after being woken by my panicky, pained wails.

'I can't. It hurts!' I rubbed the leg frantically.

'You've got to calm yourself down,' John called more quietly. 'Just try to relax and the pain will go away.'

'No it *won't*, I've got to push the muscle back *in*.'

'No, you don't, just let go of your leg and take a few deep breaths. Try it, for Godsake.'

What did I have to lose?

He was right. Within seconds the muscle relaxed and my body bathed in relief.

In the dark of this morning in Nepal, heeding that advice again, I felt the spasm start to loosen.

In the room next door an alarm clock went off loudly. The walls of the guesthouse must have been wafer thin.

Three bleary-eyed people, all struggling to wake themselves up, sat eating quietly.

'Today we start upwards,' Mani said.

'Upwards,' I moaned. 'You said today would be easier than yesterday.'

'Today not so bad as yesterday, but first uphill and then up, down, up, down. Not so bad and also jungle today.'

Akio got excited. 'Ah, jungle, I like it! Maybe we will see monkeys!'

'You like monkeys?' I asked, slightly bemused.

'In Japan my brother has a pet monkey. I like it very much.'

It's not everyday that you talk to somebody about their brother's pet monkey.

Akio wrote into his notebook, which he had placed beside him. He must have noticed my curiosity.

'I am student. I keep journal so I not-o forget,' he explained.

'Do you have a camera?'

'Camera good-o but I think journal better. Camera cannot take picture of man I hear screaming on this morning!'

The penny dropped and I must have blushed. I smiled and then turned away from him.

I sipped my milk tea; it was hot and had too much cinnamon in it. Mani rose from the table and announced that we would leave in five minutes. Again

I sipped my tea. I had packed earlier, and was under no pressure now. Despite my lowered gaze, I could feel Akio staring at me oddly.

'Is something the matter? I finally looked up and asked, trying not to sound hostile.

'Yes, no problem.'

He glanced away but I noticed that he was still very much in thought. I decided to get it over with him; surely even he had had a cramp before.

'You look as though there's something on your mind.'

'Okay, I have been-o thinking —' He fell silent again.

'Yes, what?'

'Today we might meet bandits!'

Relief. 'Don't worry about bandits,' I said breezily. Everything will be fine. You have nothing to worry about!'

Akio regarded me seriously; obviously I had interrupted too soon. He had something more to say.

'I not-o worry about bandits. What I think is, when we meet bandits today, I not want to give money.'

'You what?'

'Bandits no good-o.' He became more confident, more focused. I could tell from his tone that he felt determined about what he was saying. 'It is not a donation, they rob us. I not want to be robbed so I no want to give my money!'

Obviously he had a point — and one that I agreed with. Donating at gunpoint sounded more like robbery than charity to me. But if they had guns I was going to give them whatever they wanted. The Maoists didn't scare me off the trek but I wasn't planning on messing with them either. Years of travelling up and down to Northern Ireland had taught me that it was better to avoid confrontation; do as they asked and go home.

'Akio, I think you should give them what they want.' I spoke softly but with purpose. 'It won't be very much money to us,' I continued, 'and I think it's better to be safe than sorry.'

Akio remained calm, his tiny eyes staring at me intently. I saw that he was trying to size me up, trying to calculate whether it was worth arguing with me. Whether I could be persuaded to stand up with him against the rebels.

'We will see,' he eventually replied. 'I will think about it today while we walk.'

I wasn't satisfied. Sure, it was every man for himself, but I knew too well that in such situations it was better to be united. The fact that I'd give a donation would be entirely outweighed by Akio's reluctance. We'd be seen as one defiant unit. And Akio had probably never known the kind of violence that a terrorist group could mete out to those who resisted.

I wanted to shake some sense into him. Make him see the danger. Make him see it my way. *Listen here. You'll keep your mouth shut and give them whatever the hell they want or you can piss off.*

It's amazing how fantastic your imagination can make things look, especially a confrontation. I remembered back to when I was in primary school and I was being bullied by a boy older than me and twice my size. I told my parents and they advised me to confront him.

'Don't run away from him,' Dad instructed. 'Talk to him, tell him to leave you alone.'

For the rest of that night I'd thought of different conversations I could have with the bully, and before I fell asleep I had planned an entire speech.

The following day in the schoolyard I walked up to the boy. I was terribly nervous as I recited the speech in my head.

'What do you want?' he growled.

I was petrified. The words I'd practised just vanished from my mind. Suddenly I did what I never thought I would do — I lunged forward and kicked him between the legs. The bully collapsed to the ground. My look of astonishment must have lasted all day.

For now, I decided to let things lie with Akio. Time out. I was irritated though — and overcome by an urgent need to pray and rub my hands together. I began repeatedly brushing one palm roughly over the top of the other. *Dear God …* It was a familiar action to me but to another it would have looked absurd — as though I was desperately trying to remove some imperceptible affliction from my hands.

'What you doing?'

I turned away from Akio, trying to conceal my embarrassment. 'Nothing,' I muttered. 'Just trying to think of something.' It was a pretty lame excuse, but I'd been using it for years and it had always seemed to work.

'But, with your hands, why you do that?' Suddenly it wasn't me directing him; I was the child now.

'I…' I *what*? What kind of stupid excuse can you give now, Sean?

I was exposed. There he was, this forthright little man I hardly knew, catching me off guard in the most uncomfortable of ways.

Have I questioned him about any of his peculiarities? Why should he ask me about mine? Why should I feel the need to defend myself!

'I thought I felt a leech on my fingers. I was wiping them clean!' How practised I was at feigning — lying. It was the easiest route. Pathetic.

'Ah, I see.'

He probably thought I was some kind of weirdo.

'We leave now!' Mani's voice came like a rescuing hand over the side of a cliff. 'Yes, I think it's time!'

I leapt up.

'Ah yes, good-o, I think we make good time if we leave now.' Akio spoke pleasantly and without any hint that he was still curious. Maybe he believed me.

Mani threw my backpack upon his shoulders and we were on our way. It was a cold morning, not unlike a winter's morning back home in Ireland. A shroud of wispy clouds crossed our path and the night's rain added its own slippery touch. Yesterday the weather had been warm and heavy — quite a contrast to the cool and wintry feel now on day two. Thirty minutes into the trek, though, and despite the pinching cold, all three of us were sweating. The path still led uphill. It was, in fact, a continuation of the three thousand steps of the previous evening. It was a strenuous start to the day.

Soon Mani found a dry spot to put the backpack down. Everybody was pleased with the break, even though we'd only been walking a short time.

'Not so easy now!' Mani massaged his calf muscles. 'But later not so bad.'

Akio nodded in agreement, still wiping the sleep from his eyes. I just gazed out across the vast, vibrant landscape.

The previous day's trekking had loosened my muscles and I didn't feel so fatigued this morning. And it wouldn't be unlike me to find some competitive energy, too, with Akio joining our group. Ever since I was a kid I'd striven to be the best at everything, from athletics to music to how many pints of beer I could drink. Relentlessly, I'd pushed myself, often beyond my capabilities, especially against someone I didn't know well. But trying to be the winner was never my drive: it was the desire to let people know what I could do.

Mani was back on his feet. So was Akio. I went ahead a few steps. It felt good to be leading the group.

'You know,' she said with a giggle as we strolled along the beach, 'you walk very fast.'

'Do you think so?'

She pinched my side. 'You know so!'

Suddenly she stopped in her tracks. It was almost sundown, the beach was quiet and still, the Indian Ocean shushed calmly alongside us.

'Isn't this sunset breathtaking!' she exclaimed in a gasp of emotion.

Our footprints were still visible along the shoreline, under the intense reds, oranges and yellows of the sky. We stood side by side, hand in hand, watching the horizon and the daylight fading. Then the night sky was upon us. We didn't speak for some time. We were both happy to breathe in the cool air and enjoy the surroundings. 'You know,' she exclaimed cheerfully, 'if you don't slow down, you might just walk by a moment like this.'

Perhaps she was right. I was moving so fast I was actually running away from things.

'How about we go and get some food,' I suggested.

'Sounds perfect to me,' she said, with a beautiful smile on her face.

The path continued uphill, occasionally dipping down much to the relief of all three of us. I found that in taking the lead I'd actually wound up quite a pace, and often I had to stop to allow Mani and Akio to catch up. Now I wasn't trying to race my way through the mountains, but had just discovered that in leading I could have some time to myself. And the prayer that Akio had witnessed earlier still needed finishing undisturbed.

Dear God …

I began thinking about the Maoists. We were getting close to Ghorepani with every step and that's where the British guy had met them. What if they did have machine guns? What if things got out of control? What if the guns went off even accidentally? What if they decided to take tourists as hostages?

Dear God …

Time went by in the blink of an eye when I was dealing with a disturbing thought or an incomplete prayer — my many different attempts at reciting a prayer properly could take so much of my attention that anything else could pass without my being aware.

'What happened?' Mani rushed up as I scrambled to my feet, embarrassed.

'I'm fine,' I said with a slight grumble. 'Not a bother.'

'What happened?'

'I don't know,' I said. 'I must have tripped over my feet.'

'Not concentrating,' laughed Akio as he reached us. 'Eyes not on road.'

'I had my eyes on the road,' I snapped back. 'I just tripped — simple. Anyone could do it.'

Mani threw me a sharp look; I was taking out on Akio what I should have been taking out on myself.

'Sorry, I didn't mean to snap.'

Akio accepted my apology humbly and gave a friendly laugh.

'Anyone fancy a break?' I said then, knowing we all did.

'Maybe we stop for lunch in the next village?' Mani became enthusiastic at the prospect. '*Dal bhat* for Mani!' He rubbed his stomach in a show of his unending love for the dish.

At the thought of food we shot off along the track. With so many downhill sections now, it was even tougher, being forever teased. Each downhill burst felt like fresh air, the muscles eased, the pain drifted away and then suddenly — bang! — an uphill slog grabbed hold of our legs and tied two giant boulders to our ankles, bringing us instantly back to earth.

As I struggled along, I couldn't shake my frustration at having tripped earlier. Rituals and prayers — they're the bane of my life, I thought with disappointment.

They've affected everything I do, everything I love, even my music for Godsake!

A flurry of memories came to mind, one eventually settling upmost.

It was a showcase I'd played for record company execs back in Ireland. Showcases are nothing special — playing to one or two people who, if truth be known, usually had little power in making decisions. Generally 'they'd be in touch'.

On this day, performing solo in a room in front of four casually dressed men, I played my heart out, singing songs that meant the world to me. I'd written them for myself, but people obviously liked them, including the four guys sitting before me.

After the set of songs the room fell silent. The men showed no reaction, then began to chat among themselves as if I wasn't there. My mind started racing with worry and doubt. Finally they stopped talking. They'd reached agreement and they returned their focus to me.

'Hi, Sean!' said one. His accent was American; his tone slightly condescending. 'You probably know who I am but, in case you don't, I'm Don Taylor.' I nodded in acknowledgement. He was a well-known record producer.

'We're delighted that you agreed to come and play for us today. We've all heard so much about you. What with the media and your gigging in Dublin, you've made quite a name for yourself over the past while, even internationally.'

'Cheers,' I said quite pleased with myself. 'I didn't know I'd spread so far.'

'You must have some friends in the States,' another interrupted. 'They sent us on your material.'

'Anyway,' Don continued, cutting across the second man, 'as I'm sure you know, this is a new venture for our companies. It isn't usual that four major recording companies will come together to promote one artist.'

Cool, I thought, totally uninterested in the patter. I didn't care about the current tide of the music industry or any of the other corporate talk that music execs spewed on about. All I wanted to know was how he liked the music.

'I must tell you, we liked what we heard today. We liked it a lot.' All four smiled in agreement.

'Your music is awesome, man.' Don suddenly drifted from formal to I'm-with-the-band! 'The only problem we have is with *you*.'

I liked it better when he was praising me. I had to allow time for the information to compute. 'Me!' I exclaimed. I had been inflated and popped in a matter of seconds. 'What do you mean, me?'

'You don't look good. You've no image.' His tone was harsh and direct. 'Sean, what can I say?' he continued more genially. The music industry is a tough place and it takes more than a couple of good tunes to sell records.'

My grip tightened on my guitar neck. I could feel myself becoming flustered. I couldn't believe what I was hearing. The music doesn't count?

These four guys had first contacted me months earlier. In the time that followed, they'd heard my music, seen pictures of me, thrown me the odd compliment and basically told me that this showcase gig was just a formality.

Formality, my ass!

My mind raced, faster, infuriated. I'd been used. Standing in front of them, I wondered how I was supposed to respond to criticism like that. Thank them for the frank but belated appraisal? Without realising it, I began rubbing my hands and feet together. Not much in the beginning, but as they continued to stare at me I became conscious of what I was doing. I tried to stop. I tried to speak but I was in a mental freeze. No words could explain this mad action I was performing.

I clenched my fists, then loosened them. Rubbed one shoe over another and then repeated the act.

Turn your back to them. No, I can't do that, I'll look even worse.

Dear Holy God please protect …

I had to move my hand on the guitar neck. It felt as though all the negativity I'd heard was now at the tip where I was holding it. If I moved my hand the negativity would go. But before I moved it, I had to wipe the tip so that the negativity would be able to leave.

Dear Holy God please protect …

Surely I looked as though I was having a fit, but the four men continued to look on without comment.

What are they staring at? I NEED TO TURN MY BACK AND COMPOSE MYSELF.

'I need to compose myself,' I suddenly exclaimed aloud, then turned around.

Breathe. Breathe. Breathe.

There was a silence in the room that was sharp and vicious. Finally I turned back and looked at the men.

'I'm so sorry,' I exclaimed, 'I really am so sorry.'

They continued to stare at me.

'Obviously I don't take criticism easily!' I laughed nervously, trying to make light of the situation. Still the men remained quiet.

Wait a minute, why am I taking this crap from these guys? I can leave this. These guys have no hold on me. I am a free agent. What have I lost? Just a little time and ego.

I stepped down from the small stage where I'd been standing and packed away my guitar.

'Sorry to have wasted your Saturday,' I said sourly, as I made my way to the door.

Don's voice echoed from behind. 'That could work!' He spoke confidently, with excitement. I heard another voice agreeing and I turned to inquire.

'What could work?' I knew the answer before it had even left his mouth.

'That, what was it —?' He tried to describe it. 'That mental breakdown thing you just did there. The thing you did with your hands and your feet! Whatever it was you were doing, we could sell that.'

I was shocked. 'You could sell what? What are you talking about?' I bluffed.

'Even better, he doesn't even know he does it. We could definitely sell that!' Don was practically salivating at the prospect.

'I know exactly what you're talking about!' I fought back. 'My problems are not part of the deal!'

'Think about it.'

Don's words grated through my mind as I slammed the door behind me. It was misery to think that the worst in me was the only thing that could make the best of me come alive.

'Owww,' yelled Akio from behind. I had just reached our lunch village ahead of the others, but ran back to investigate.

'Leechee,' he cried. 'Look, leechee on my leg.' He pointed to the black slug-like creature sucking at his heel.

'Pull it off,' I said.

Akio reached for the leech and pulled at it with his thumb and forefinger. The leech came off with a light spurt of blood and then proceeded to stick itself to his hand, sucking instantly.

'Now it on my thumb!'

Mani came closer and began to laugh as we watched Akio trying to pick the leech off with his other hand. Each time he succeeded in removing it from one hand it stuck to the other. I found it quite amusing too, and even Akio could see the funny side of it. The leech was ruthless. Finally, with a swift attack Akio managed to lift the leech and send it flying through the air, to a location unknown to us all.

'Phew, no messing around with that leech,' I said to Akio with a chuckle.

'Ah, like a Dracula,' commented Akio, now tending to the wound on his leg.

'You have more on your shoe.' Mani pointed down towards Akio's feet. Five fat leeches were wriggling through the lace holes of his left boot.

'Ah shit-o,' he cried.

Ten minutes and five flying leeches later we were sitting at a table in a small teahouse. Mani would have *dal bhat* with the family soon. Akio and I awaited our noodle soup.

'What do you do for work?' Mani's question came unexpectedly after all this time.

'I study, eh, chemistry. Research-o,' Akio answered, waving his hands as he spoke.

'Is it good job?' Mani asked, very interested.

'It is for me a good job but, I think, not for everybody.'

Our noodle soup arrived and Akio began to slurp into his, as did I.

'You, Sean, you have good job?' Mani looked serious.

'I work on contracts — as an engineer!' I replied. 'You know, electricity!'

Damien Leith

I mimed electrocuting myself and Mani copied my action, showing he understood.

'What about you, Mani, why did you become a porter?' I had wanted to ask the question since I'd met him and now was the right time. Mani's big eyes glanced at me briefly and then he smiled shyly.

'When I was a boy, my family very poor. We not so much money.' He began to laugh; it was becoming clear that laughter was his way of easing around awkward conversation. 'In Nepal it is difficult —' he qualified this — 'I think it's very difficult.' Mani continued to talk as he looked away from Akio and me. 'I hear about porter work. My uncle was guide and he give me job. First I work for no money, only *dal bhat*. I carry bags while my uncle is guide. Now my cousin Om help bring me work and I get three hundred rupees for one week.'

'Ah, very bad-o money,' said Akio, shovelling a spoonful of noodle soup into his mouth.

I was surprised by Akio's rudeness, but Mani seemed unfazed. 'I give two hundred to my family and rest for *dal bhat* and saving. It is good, I think! Soon I work for me, I my own company.' Again Mani broke off in laughter.

When he was called for his lunch, I watched him slip away with the family and felt a mixture of sadness and cheer. You almost always meet somebody who has it ten times worse than you. Mani's three hundred rupees a week amounted to one large meal for me — or four Mars bars from a stall along the trek path. Yet it was obvious how valued he was by the families we met; always taken into their circle.

Dear Holy God, please protect Mam and Dad, John, Sarah and Sam, Benji and Rusty, all my friends and relatives and everybody who needs your help today and Mani.

How could Akio be so insensitive to such a hardworking guy?

Dear Holy God, please protect Mam and Dad, John, Sarah and Sam, Benji and Rusty, all my friends and relatives and everybody who needs your help today and Mani ... and Mani ... and Mani.

I couldn't get his name to feel right, and I needed to or his prospects would never improve. Akio slurped once again from his noodles and wrote a few notes in his book.

I rubbed my thumbs against my forefingers. *Mani ... Mani.*

I rubbed my temples and thought hard about the words. *Mani*. It worked.

I must be going mad. I can't change anything about Mani's life, it's his life.

I ate my noodles in silence. I was a dickhead.

6. *The Maoist*

We stayed at the teahouse for about half an hour.

Mani returned full of vigour and we set off again, refuelled and a lot more energetic. I took the lead as I had done earlier. After a short walk we entered jungle. It was almost as though we'd been transported to a different place entirely. All around us were trees, dense, thick and grey — real jungle, far more concentrated than forest and much more intimidating. Only a little light managed to creep in, so it was also much cooler. The path here no longer ran over large stones, but was made up of shards of fallen tree branches. Because of the rain the night before, this was terribly slippery to tread on.

Surprisingly, Mani was the first to fall. He clambered to his feet in seconds, and as of to his hide embarrassment briskly assumed the lead, while I took up the rear. Then, when we had been walking for almost two hours, Akio's foot caught on a loose piece of wood. Under the weight of his backpack he keeled over. Mani turned swiftly to respond to Akio's cry, but Akio's slight stumble had developed alarmingly — over the side of the track and into a steep drop into thick trees and shrubbery below. We could hear Akio yelling in panic as he continued to roll, hands grabbing at whatever they could find.

Under the weight of my pack Mani could gather little speed to reach him. In desperation I threw my arm over the mountainside but Akio was well gone.

'Ah shit! Shit, shit, shit,' I yelled. 'Akio! Akio!'

I peered over the edge, desperately trying to see where he'd landed. The drop below rose up, brought terrifyingly close by the vast covering of branches and leaves below the edge — he could be anywhere. Mani lay by my side, puffing and panting. We called out Akio's name, but there was no response.

'Akio, Akio,' we yelled again, but still no response.

'Where *is* he?' I asked in shock.

'I don't know, I see nothing.' Again we yelled his name; there was silence.

'Ah, this is insane!' I groaned, then tried a tremendous shout, '*AKIO!*'

'I am a here-a.' The voice was faint but there was no doubting it was Akio. Mani and I looked everywhere below the edge — but we could see no sign of him.

'He could be anywhere down there,' I said to Mani. 'There are too many leaves in the way to see a thing.'

'Where are you?' Mani cried out, giving me a signal to be very quiet. Akio's voice was just loud enough for Mani to pick the direction from which it came. 'Over there,' he said, pointing off to the right.

'I'll go down and get him,' I said rising to my feet. 'I need a rope or something. Have you got one?'

'No, I will go down.' His words were definite and direct. Perhaps this was best; Mani knew this country.

He had already removed the backpack and was making a plan to get down over the edge. At first he tried easing himself over the edge, feeling his way by his feet, but his right foot gave way and I pulled him back up.

'Rope, maybe we need rope.'

You can say that again. A prayer surfaced horribly in my mind as I rummaged through the jungle trying to find something that resembled a rope. *Dear Holy God, please protect Mam, Dad, John, Sarah and Sam, Benji and Rusty, all my friends and relatives, Mani, and Akio hanging off the cliff.*

Again and again I repeated the prayer, and although my fingers and toes aimed to the sky as much as they could, I was unable to get it right! This was hopeless. *Akio could die!*

'There, at your feet.' Mani spoke but I was too slow to respond. Not until he was tugging at a large heap of vine-like branches beneath me, did I even see them.

Damn prayers! I felt stupid and angry. And distressed. Now my *scolding* of the prayers could be the cause of Akio's falling further and perhaps even dying. I continued to recite the lines in my head as I helped Mani to tie the vine rope around a tree and go over the edge. But then, just as Mani began to descend, Akio called out his name.

With neither Mani nor I noticing, Akio had somehow begun to climb up a vine that hung naturally over the edge to the ground below. Now, with strong tugs and a great deal of energy, he succeeded in coming to his own rescue. Eventually he was standing beside us.

'Ah, you two, not fast enough!' He began to dust himself down triumphantly. 'You two like big girls.'

Mani smiled briefly in relief and took up a squatting position. I wasn't sure if his look was in pain or dismay.

* * *

Akio had hurt himself in the fall and rubbed his head tentatively. I assumed he had been knocked unconscious for some seconds, probably while we called his name. Once he was awake again, it was like nothing had ever happened; he simply climbed back up to the path — in the same strange way a rain shower in Ireland arrives, creates panic, and almost as quickly disappears like nothing ever happened. Nevertheless, we took it easy for the remainder of the walk to Ghorepani. It took much longer than we had hoped, but we made it there in one piece.

The sight of Ghorepani village ahead in the distance revived us all. It was a much larger version of all the other villages we had encountered along the way — the same stony buildings, the same corrugated blue roofs.

The same, except for the atmosphere. Everywhere else we'd passed through, whether big or small, still managed to give an impression of openness, a welcome-to-the-public feel. Ghorepani was the opposite. A sign read, '*Welcome to Ghorepani*,' but the faces said, 'Go away while you still can.'

I half expected a tumbleweed to roll by.

'Somebody must be dead,' Akio suddenly exclaimed.

'I don't think so,' I replied. It wasn't that kind of atmosphere; it was more one of fear.

Eerily, for such a large village, not many villagers seemed to be outside their front doors. Occasionally a pair of eyes could be seen peeking from a slit in a curtain, or there'd be that feeling of someone present, of being watched from behind. Even Mani, a fellow Nepalese, couldn't resist turning sideways, with a glance or two.

The hotel that Mani preferred here was the Basecamp and, true to his previous form, it was at the highest point in the village, which was yet a further ten minutes away. Steadily, we made our way through the cobbled, barren streets until we were within metres of our final destination.

'Hello, I represent the Maoist. Where you come from?'

Akio let out a slight scream. The fellow *had* appeared from nowhere. He was a short Nepalese man, young, sallow-skinned, dressed in casual clothes and, most noticeably, brandishing a machine gun over his shoulder. It was surprising how attention-getting the weapon was: I just couldn't take my eyes off it. Each time I told myself to stop looking at the gun, I'd redirect my attention to his face, but almost as quickly

I'd be drawn back to its menacing, steely shape. It was mesmerising.

Mani took control of the conversation, in English.

'We travel to base camp, come from Ulleri.'

Dear Holy God, please protect — Start again.

'You stay in Basecamp Hotel tonight?' the man asked, eyeing Akio and me inquisitively.

Dear Holy God, please protect ... please protect ... ple ... please protect ... Can't get it right! *Please protect ...* Start again ... *Dear Holy God, please protect ...*

'Yes, we stay in Basecamp tonight.' Mani spoke confidently. I was trying to listen but I had to get the words right or who knows what would happen to us.

... Please protect, Mam, Dad ... Damn, not right! *... Mam, Dad ... please protect Mam, Dad, John, Sarah and Sam ...* the feeling isn't right ... *Sam ...* still not right ... *Sam ...* Shit, say the damn word *right.*

Akio said something that I didn't hear. I might have looked as though I was present in their conversation but my mind was at war for their protection.

... Please protect Mam, Dad, John, Sarah and Sam, Benji and Rusty, all my friends and relatives, Mani and Akio, especially Mani and Akio and me right now with the Maoist ... with the ... can't seem to get it right, *with the Maoist ... Mao ...*

Suddenly everybody was staring at me. There was something I'd missed. What was it? Something they wanted from me. A deathly silence hung over us, and even my mind seemed to be quelled at just that moment.

'What?' I said nervously. I had to say something; the look on Mani's face was beckoning me to speak.

'You do not understand me?' The Maoist seemed genuinely concerned, which, for a terrorist with a machine gun, I thought, was a little surprising.

'Yes, yes, I can understand you. Sorry, I was just ...'

I let the sentence hang in such a manner as to imply that I was trying to find simple words to explain myself. He took the bait and, obliged to repeat the question, asked more impatiently, 'Where you come from, what *country*?'

... *Please protect Mam, Dad.*

'I come from Ireland!'

... *John, Sarah, Sam, Benji* ...

'Ah, football in Ireland, right?' He made a kicking motion with his leg; the machine gun swayed randomly.

Fingers aiming upwards, not so much that anyone might suspect, as fast as possible I continued the recitation: *and Rusty, all my friends and relatives, Mani and Akio, especially Mani, Akio and me right now with the Maoist.*

Success! Cheerfully I could answer, 'Yes, right, football land, we play lots of football in Ireland.'

'I like football, I like it a lot!' His statement hung for a moment and then an awkward silence descended again, we three awaiting his next move.

'Okay,' he said in a jovial tone and with a clap of his hands, 'maybe I come see you all later in Basecamp Hotel. Maybe you like to help with a donation, yes?'

We simply stared back at him.

The preliminaries were over. With a slight step backwards the gunman let us pass and we made our way towards the Basecamp.

There was always a chance that we would meet the Maoists, everybody had told us that we would. But like most things in life, nobody ever wants to greet bad news until it's sitting in their laps.

We entered the hotel deflated.

'Ah, not good-o,' Akio mumbled as he threw his backpack on the wooden floor of the guesthouse.

'No, not good at all,' I agreed.

'There is nothing to worry about,' said Mani, still confident. 'Later he will come for money. Give him money and then he leave, no problem.'

No problem, as long as Akio stuck to that plan.

Akio caught my questioning look and turned suddenly to Mani to ask where the bedrooms were.

Mani caught the attention of a fine-looking Nepalese woman I took to be the wife of the owner. She was pretty, with that rare, natural beauty often sought by women back home in lotions, moisturisers and facial creams, which pharmaceutical giants present as miracle products. Her jet-black hair was long, straight and tied back from her face, while her figure was slim and attractively delicate. Despite her beauty it was difficult to overlook a certain hardness in her, as she roughly shooed away a couple of small children who peered out from behind a curtained-off room.

'This is Jagan, our host,' Mani introduced her. Then, instead of seeking out her husband, Mani entered straight into negotiations about prices and rooms. Business concluded, Jagan withdrew to her kitchen and Mani showed us around the house.

'Where is Jagan's husband?' I asked Mani, curious at finding a woman undertaking the business side of things.

'No husband,' Mani replied. 'Husband die in big fire. This new home. Her old home burn down two years ago with baby inside. Husband go in to save baby, but he die. She widow now and not much money. Plenty bad luck for Jagan. No one to look after her.'

Back in the living area we could hear her small children now playing in the kitchen behind the curtain. To think that such misfortune could befall this young family! A wife without her husband, children without their father, and a lifetime of insecurity and hard work. It was sobering.

We decided on turns in the shower. I was first.

'I think the shower might be little cold,' Mani hinted as I made my way there, towel and clean clothes in hand.

'I don't care,' I replied. 'I'll take anything that'll even half wash this day from me.'

I stood naked beneath that icy shower, the blast of water teasing already aching skin, and shrieked my arse off. If anyone heard, they would have thought that I'd lost my mind, but it seemed the natural thing to do. Bollock naked in one of the poorest countries in the world, at an altitude that was too high to support reliable electricity, in a town overrun with terrorists — and my only real concern was for a hot shower. When the shrieks had subsided I imagined myself cooling down, on a hot beach somewhere in Africa.

Harold's Bay was the place, a small beach hidden quietly away along the garden route at the base of South Africa. With huge cliffs either side, Harold's Bay was our family's favourite beach when I was a kid, and we went there every week. We had moved to South Africa for my dad's work, and I think he took to the lifestyle better than anyone else. He loved South Africa, especially Harold's Bay. Even in winter Dad took us there. He adored the water and often spent hours out swimming, letting his working week drift away.

With our Irish skin, the summer sun made it too hot to stay baking on the sand, and the ocean was the best retreat to cool off in. Wading contentedly in that deep blue sea, I'd think of Ireland, where it would be winter. And afterwards, on cold nights back home in Ireland, or winter's days standing at a bus shelter hoping that the next bus wouldn't be full already, memories of that beautiful place could always transport the senses to a different plane — just as they did today, again, in Nepal.

'How was the water?' asked Akio as I emerged from the shower.

'Lovely,' I replied without hesitation.

When I heard the gush of shower water and Akio's loud girlish scream, I smiled to myself.

In the living area of the teahouse, Mani was in deep conversation with an elderly Nepalese man. They were standing together, speaking Nepali, but stopped as soon as I entered the room. The other man turned to look at me.

'You from Ireland?' he asked. 'I have good friend from Ireland.' He was a short, portly man, with a weathered face and a slight limp which showed as he approached me.

'He from Kerry,' he said. 'I help him when he trek here.' From his pocket he pulled out a wallet and, after a moment of searching through various pieces of paper, he presented me with a tear-out from an envelope. Handwritten on it was 'William Clancy, Tralee, Co. Kerry'.

'Ah, this is your friend,' I said, trying to sound interested.

'Yes, he sometime write me, he sometime send me money. We both good friends, maybe someday I go to Ireland to meet with him again.'

'Ah, very nice.' His mention of money increased my reserve. But there was nowhere to hide.

'When my friend was here in Nepal, he fall very badly. It was winter. I am masseur, all types! Every evening I come around to each teahouse in Ghorepani, offer my services. That night he was here.'

It was amazing how his English improved as the conversation progressed! Within no time at all I had heard the entire story: how William injured his leg in a dreadful fall and how the man massaged his leg back to perfect health and then guided William back down the mountain to the comfort of Pokhara.

'Ever since then, we been good friends,' he continued.

'That's brilliant,' I said, trying to give an impression of sincerity. An awkward silence followed, during which I could sense that the man wanted me to say something — like 'Maybe I could do with a massage!' or 'What would one of those marvellous massages cost?' Instead I sat down and began to set up a game of solitaire with my miniature playing cards. Mani noticed the silence and took on a daydreaming air. But blatantly ignoring somebody was never my way of doing things. A part of me felt guilty.

The masseur broke the impasse. 'You have had a long day walking, maybe you would like a massage, very cheap price?'

'Ah, it's okay,' I said pleasantly, trying not to hurt his feelings. 'Thanks for the offer, but my muscles feel good today.' I squeezed happily on my calf for effect, to show him how supple they were. He seemed resigned with this. I, on the other hand, was secretly surprised at how much pain I'd squeezed out.

'Okay,' he sighed reluctantly. 'So you feel good today. That is good!' He looked about the room and then returned his attention to me. 'I hope you enjoy Nepal and I am happy to meet another Irishman. I like Irish very much.'

Just at that moment Akio emerged from his shower, fresh and dressed, his hair wet and fuzzy.

'Oh you trick-o me,' he said, wagging a finger in my direction. 'Water very cold!'

I considered explaining about Africa and the ocean, but since he saw humour in it, I let it go.

'Next time I trick-o you. Next time my turn.'

'You from Japan?' the masseur addressed him. I watched with interest. Akio hesitated before answering. 'Yes, but I no interested in massage.'

How could he have known the man's intentions? Perhaps he'd overheard us; on the other hand, I was learning that Akio was strangely resourceful.

'You have met me before?' The masseur, too, was surprised and I could tell he was now curious about Akio.

Akio held a towel in his hand and began to dry his hair as he spoke, barely making eye contact with the man. 'We not meet but I know what you are selling because I read about men like you in my books.'

'I am a good man.' The masseur became emotional. 'I mean you no harm!'

'I know you are man in business,' interrupted Akio. 'That is why I am honest with you. Massage is not for me tonight.' The finality in his words was unarguable and the masseur was clearly defeated.

'Good night.' He nodded at Akio and again at me before leaving the house.

It was just after six o'clock. The evening had come upon us fast. In the dark outside a dense fog had enveloped the teahouse and added to the blackness. I continued my games of solitaire, while Mani stretched out and Akio entertained himself with a book. All of us awaited our evening meal.

In the content atmosphere that had settled over us, any niggling dread of the Maoist's expected return was invisible. Shortly after seven, pastimes discarded,

Jagan served us our meals. While Akio and I ate, she and Mani spoke quietly to one another in Nepali.

'Do you like?' she suddenly asked in clear English, her words directed at me.

I hadn't eaten much yet, too distracted with watching the children and their mother. Her personal tragedy continued to play on my mind.

I smiled. 'Yes, it's lovely.'

She nodded her head, but her lips pouted in a way not uncommon among disapproving teachers.

'I can make you something else,' she persisted. In all my time in India and Nepal, never once had somebody volunteered to replace a meal with something else. Every meal would have been the equivalent of a day's earnings to whoever served it.

'No, honestly, it's lovely.' I began to fork food into my mouth to show my fondness for the dish, perhaps overdoing it a little. But she seemed to get the message and returned her attention to Mani, who strangely wasn't making much headway either with his beloved *dal bhat*.

'Mine is not so good-o. Many lumps!' Akio raised the spoon from his bowl to show how badly the yellow liquid flowed. It was true that the meal wasn't as fluid as it should have been, but I was shocked by

Akio's unkindness. Who eats custard with potato soup anyway?

Jagan immediately sprang to her feet, took the bowl of custard with a smile and told Akio that she would replace it. I was overcome by a rush of embarrassment, then anger. It wasn't the first time that day that Akio had acted insultingly with a Nepalese person. The Nepalese I'd met were humble, modest people. Akio wasn't in any way sensitive to his environment, I thought. He knew this woman's circumstances, and a quick glance around the interior of her teahouse would tell anyone that this family wasn't in a position to be throwing food away; it just wasn't an option.

'Did you really have to complain about the custard?' I whispered. 'It wasn't that bad.'

'I no like,' he replied, screwing up his face for effect.

'But you'd eaten nearly all of it!' I continued. 'You had hardly any left!'

'But I no like, not so good-o. Better I complain so next time she make much better.' Akio remained entirely focused as he spoke, exhibiting no aggression in his words; he was simply stating what he believed to be true.

My brother John had been just like this when we were kids. As I finished off the food that remained on my plate, I thought of those childish fusses — skirmishes that evolved from thin air and almost always resulted in a full-blown argument. But fighting with John had never gone in my favour. I would want to shout the issue out, while John would take the calm approach, uttering only what was necessary and, mostly, what was correct. And the calmer he was, the more frustrated I became — which only ended up handing him the ultimate blow: 'Calm down, you're acting like a kid, you're acting like your baby brother Sam.' Those words were decisive and didn't leave an opening for a comeback.

John knew that the only thing I ever wanted when I was a kid was to be an adult. While everybody else hoped to become a *fireman* or a *pilot* when they were older, I just wanted to be Adult. Maybe it was because my parents always looked so secure to me. Adulthood seemed to allow them the opportunity to have what they wanted, when they wanted it, and to be entirely safe in their unity. The unending bills, the secret arguments, the drudge of working every day to get the kids through school and to buy the week's groceries — these were always pushed out of sight, so I could live with the notion that it all became easier when you got older.

*　　*　　*

Jagan returned with Akio's custard, which he received with a jovial, 'Thank-o you.' She began preparing her young children for bed. Mani and I both finished eating, and while he sat daydreaming, I began my fifth unsuccessful game of solitaire.

There was a loud knock on the front door. Everybody knew who it was, but still we each looked around in the direction of the door, hoping that it might be somebody different. It wasn't. He let himself in, bringing with him a stinging gust of cool night air which dissipated slowly as the door shut behind him. Jagan calmly ushered her children out of the room towards the kitchen, and Mani, Akio and I sat nervously, waiting to see what would unfold.

The man looked at us individually for a few moments. We each remained silent. Abruptly he turned to Mani and, with a cheerful smile, asked if he could sit down.

'Don't worry about this —' He placed his machine gun on the floor beside him. 'It is not such a safe time for people like me now. We need protection.' How strangely the atmosphere in the room had been transformed: with his arrival came the bleakness of the night that up until then we'd been so well sheltered from.

'Okay,' he sighed resignedly. 'I said I would come tonight and so here I am — I am an honest man.' His words seemed to dangle expectantly in the air, as though they were expecting some kind of rebuttal; instead they scrambled away unmet. Each person was waiting to see what the other was going to do.

Mani broke the tension, saying something to the man in Nepali. Akio and I watched. The two men talked almost normally with one another. This was comforting. There didn't appear to be any danger. Finally the two men broke off their conversation and the Maoist representative turned to Akio and me.

'My name is Raja. What are your names?'

Akio was as forward as ever. 'I am, eh, Akio.'

'Yeah, and I'm Sean,' I mumbled, painfully, silently reciting a prayer.

'Sean and Akio, good.' He reached into his trouser pocket and presented us with a pencilled document. 'As you know, I am a representative of the Maoist,' he explained. 'We are fighting for the common man in Nepal and we look for donations from people like you two. That piece of paper that I give you is a letter from very high up in the Maoist organisation, please read.'

Akio read aloud: 'Dear Tourist, We are the Maoist communist party. We wish for one donation of R1000 from every tourist to help our fight. We fight for the common Nepalese, the poor Nepalese. We need donation to help with medical, to help with food. We ask that you give donation and if you wish not to, we remind you that you still have long travels ahead of you. Thank you.'

The message was clear — give money or there'd be trouble. My mind tripped over its attempts at prayer.

'You both understand?' Raja's words were directed particularly towards me. He could see I was distracted, agitated.

'Yes, we understand. But —' I paused for a second. 'One thousand rupees is a lot of money. We've come up the mountains with only enough for our trek. Is it okay if we give a little less?' The words had left my mouth before I'd considered what I was saying. But clearly I'd struck the right thing. Raja looked at me questioningly for a short while and then asked how much I was willing to give. I felt fantastic, powerful — for that brief moment my mind was totally clear of any promises, of any prayers. Earlier I had decided that I would give the Maoists whatever they wished, no questions asked, but all that had suddenly changed, with one confident reply. I could name my price now — but I was still aware of how volatile the situation was. Five hundred rupees seemed a fair sum. Raja stared at me again while he contemplated the offer.

'Okay, five hundred rupees is not such a bad donation.' He spoke slowly, considering. 'If you get money for me now, I will write you receipt so you don't have to pay Maoist if you meet them again.'

Raja produced a receipt book and began writing while Akio and I rummaged through our wallets and I handed over my money. Raja gave me a receipt. But then the situation changed.

'I will not-o pay!' Akio was looking through his wallet as he spoke. Did he not have five hundred rupees? He put away the wallet and reiterated, 'I will not-o pay.'

Even Mani couldn't believe his ears. 'I think it is better that you give small donation,' he said firmly.

'I will not-o pay. I am sorry, I do not support the Maoist.'

Raja rose from his chair and looked down at Akio. It was clear that he wasn't sure how to proceed. He sat back down again. After some reflection, he spoke impatiently.

'It is best that you give small donation as I think you have much travel left and you do not want to make enemies along the way.'

Mani and I stared, intrigued, nervous.

'You terrorist, you bandit,' Akio continued coolly. 'I not support you or your fight. Not my problem.' He prodded a thumb against his chest. 'Not my problem!' The words had determination ringing all the way through them.

Raja knew that too. With a massive lunge, he leapt from his chair towards Akio. Both men fell to the floor with a crash, Raja on top, gripping tightly around Akio's neck. In uproar, Raja shouted as Akio struggled beneath him. Mani rushed to the panicking family in the kitchen.

Instinctively I began pulling at Raja to break up the fight. Raja kept his tight hold around Akio's neck, and as I tried to separate the two of them I glimpsed the fury on Raja's face, the utter focus on harming this defiant tourist.

Suddenly a crying child emerged from the kitchen and ran towards us, her mother behind her being held back by Mani. The child began to shout something in Nepali, smacking at both Raja and me with her tiny hands, obviously trying to put an end to the commotion, obviously thinking that I was attacking Akio too. With a swift swing of his right arm, Raja threw the little girl to the ground and almost as fast

regained hold of Akio. I could hear the child scream —
she had landed on her back, her head following with a
hard thump on the wooden floor. Enraged, I threw a
heavy fist into Raja's face. He released his grip on
Akio. With a tremendous tug I pulled Raja off then fell
backwards, landing not far from the little girl.

For a moment the room was still. Raja was
standing, Akio was on the ground wheezing for air,
and I lay dazed beside the whimpering child. In the
background I could hear the muffled sobs of Jagan.

Raja looked around the room, first at Akio, then at
the girl and finally at me. He brought his attention
back to the child; a look of pain crossed his face as he
saw he had hurt her. He muttered something gruffly to
Jagan then collected himself and picked up his gun.
Slowly he walked towards Akio, stopping inches away
from him but making no eye contact, his machine gun
by his side aimed loosely towards Akio.

'All I wanted was a donation, but now everything is
no good!' He crouched down beside Akio and spoke
directly to him, occasionally looking in my direction.
'We are poor people here in Nepal. I am family man. I
love my wife and my children. Do you think that I do
this for fun? No! I would rather be with them, not here
with you.' His voice was emotional. 'But this is a war.

You think it is not your problem, but when you come to a country that is at war, then it is your problem. All I wanted is donation and now instead I have to do something about this.'

Silence followed.

'What will you do?' Akio spoke then, out of sheer nerves, the colour slowly returning to his face.

Raja rose to his feet and began to walk towards the door. 'What will you do?' shouted Akio again. 'Tell me.'

Raja opened the door, the cool night air once again stampeding into the room, catching hold of everybody, adding to the strain.

'Tomorrow morning, you —' he pointed at Akio, and then pointed at me '— and you — we will be waiting for you both.'

'Us *both*?' I shouted. 'What the hell did I do? I gave you my money.' But Raja was gone, and though I shouted after him from the door, he did not return. I went back into the room vexed, my mind in turmoil.

'You're a prick, Akio.'

Akio climbed to his feet and then sat down. Mani was attending the distressed family, who were feverishly hugging the hurt child. I marched up and down the room.

Dear Holy God, please protect — What was Akio thinking? *Dear Holy God, please pro* — I saved the prick's life, what was he thinking? — *Dear Holy* —

I couldn't get my mind around what had just taken place.

'Thank-o you, thank-o you for saving me.' Akio nearly whispered the words, as if he was ashamed of what had happened. He kept his head low.

'What are we going to *do*?' I said desperately. 'What's going to happen tomorrow?'

I put my hand to my forehead and found that my head was bleeding from the fall. Mani entered the room. He said nothing but the expression on his face was enough.

'Mani, what will we do?' I had to ask him, even if he had no ideas, just to feel that we weren't on our own.

Mani thought for a short while and eventually replied, 'We better sleep, leave very early tomorrow.'

'How early?' I enquired.

'Maybe five, maybe more early but I think we must sleep soon.' My mind began to relax. I hadn't completed the prayer but it wasn't nagging at me as much.

'Is the little girl okay?'

'She is good, not so bad.' Mani began to laugh sympathetically while over-exaggeratedly flexing his arm muscles. 'She is strong, very brave girl.'

I wiped away a streak of blood that had dripped down my neck. 'Okay, I'm off to bed.'

I passed by Akio but refused to look at him.

The last I remember of the hours of murmuring that night was lying deathly still, fingers flexed tightly in upright positions, my feet and toes stretched as far upwards as they possibly could. It was supremely uncomfortable but it was the only remedy for my distressed mind.

7. *On the run*

'Wake up, wake up.' Mani's words penetrated my sleep with urgency. Like a person brought back to life, I awoke in a panic. Mani was actually in my room!

He retreated from my bedside. 'I am sorry, but we must go soon! You sleep deep, I cannot wake you for a long time.'

The previous night's events flooded back into my mind.

'Okay, I'm awake.' I threw a leg out from the bed and onto the cold wooden floor.

'Good, we leave as soon as possible.' Mani turned and scurried out of the room.

I hauled the rest of my body from beneath the sheets. Because of the bitter cold, I was dressed and ready to leave within minutes, and soon entered the living area of the teahouse, where Mani was waiting. He was so anxious to leave he already had my backpack on.

'Is Akio ready?' I asked, anxious to leave too.

'Akio not want to come with us!' Mani replied curtly.

'He what?' I was taken aback. 'Is he not awake?'

'He awake, but he say he want breakfast before he leave.'

I was instantly furious. Had Akio forgotten the mess he'd managed to get us all embroiled in?

'I'll sort him out!'

I stormed to Akio's room. He was sitting up reading the trek map with a pocket torch that he held in one hand. He looked as though he'd been awake for some time.

'Come on, get up and let's get going!' I tugged at his blankets. But Akio held them tight, intent on staying in bed.

'Why aren't you coming?' I asked in frustration.

'I not-o frightened of Maoist. They all mouth.' Akio gestured flapping lips with his right hand. 'I wait for breakfast and then I leave. I leave when I am ready!'

I could hardly comprehend his smugness. He had nearly been throttled last night! Didn't he believe they were serious? Perhaps he thought his rights as a customer would be compromised if he didn't get the breakfast he was owed. This was madness. Now I wanted to be as far away from him as possible.

Nevertheless, I pleaded with him. 'Akio, I honestly think that you should come with us now. You don't know what you're dealing with.'

Akio regarded me for a moment and then grinned slyly. 'Ah, you very frightened of Maoist and I think this might be problem for you, because maybe you not so good-o in your head.'

What?

He went on. 'I see you many times, you sick-o with your head.'

'Hey, Akio, you know what, you can go get stuffed for all I care.' And I left the room before he could reply.

Sick-o in the head. Who does he think he is? Who the hell does that smug imbecile think he is to talk to me like that?

If Mani had heard what passed between Akio and me he said nothing. He picked up my pack and headed for the door, knowing I was following now and Akio was no longer a concern for either of us.

The freezing morning air hit us with the same implacable force as Akio's attitude. Each breath we took was dragged in, then left our mouths as a puff of fog under the still moonlit early-morning sky. The houses we passed seemed lost under the darkness, and peaceful, but the village of Ghorepani, still harboured a threat, which wouldn't pass until this place was no longer in sight. We didn't speak to one another. We stayed focused on the path before us. Akio's last words replayed in my head over and over again. Who was he to judge me? At least I had never put our lives in danger. Yet his accusations stung. I was angry — and embarrassed.

Then the image of the Nepalese child being pushed to the ground came to me — she had suffered because she had tried to come to Akio's aid. Why didn't that appear to bother him?

I couldn't make sense of what Akio had done and I couldn't clear it from my mind either. Perhaps he didn't have any money. If that was the case, I could have helped him out. A whisper kept surfacing in my mind — the Maoists would catch up with Akio and put a bullet through his thick skull. What a disaster!

Again I was lured into frustrating prayers: if something happened to Akio then maybe my thinking ill of him would be to blame.

Dear Holy God, please keep Akio safe and okay and alive and well and in good health …

The words churned over in my mind with no sense of completion, refused like an incorrect pin number punched into an ATM. My prayers were becoming increasingly difficult to recite.

Sunrise began to decorate the sky and Ghorepani was already far behind. We had been walking for over an hour, but I had been too preoccupied with my mental rituals to notice time or distance. No matter what route the words ran though the canals of my head they never seemed right — yet if I didn't complete the prayer properly, Akio would most certainly die! At last I shut my eyes. I had no choice. Too many surrounding objects were distracting me. Anything aiming down represented badness. Simple things such as a bird coming down to land meant I had to start the prayer again. Maybe its descent represented hell and damnation — that my prayer was plunging to depths not rising to heaven. Whatever. Eyes shut, fingers and toes flexed into the upward position, I began this new prayer one more time.

Dear Holy God, please keep Akio safe and okay and alive and well and in good health …

The concentration involved was immense, but this time it worked, the words flowed out without a problem. Success!

I opened my eyes with renewed enthusiasm, hoping that Mani hadn't seen. He hadn't, but I hadn't observed him either —

'Oh, shit, Mani?' I shouted as I ran towards him. Up ahead he'd curled over on bent knees. His face was screwed up in agony, his hands were pressing tightly to his stomach.

'Here, take that off your shoulders,' I cried, undoing the fasteners and releasing my pack from his tiny frame.

'No problem,' he moaned. 'Only little pain.'

I threw the backpack to one side and tried to see what was wrong with him. Perhaps he'd fallen while I'd had my eyes shut. But on closer inspection, he looked as though he'd suffered some kind of attack.

'Where's the pain?'

Mani pointed to his stomach.

'Your stomach. What's wrong, what are you feeling, do you want to head back?'

'It's nothing. I have pain with my stomach, it's no problem.' He started to crawl to his feet but I stopped him. He clearly wasn't ready to stand.

'Don't get up. Sit down here for a while, catch your breath!' I helped him over to a large boulder, somewhere he could sit safe from leeches. His face had become sickly pale and he was out of breath.

'Okay, now breathe slowly.' He looked past me, still in the grip of pain, but did as I suggested. 'Alright, now tell me, what exactly are you feeling?'

Mani thought for a second. With each breath the colour was returning to his face, surprisingly fast. 'I think it is not so bad now. My stomach I think sometimes not so happy with me.' I smiled at this and couldn't help but think about all the *dal bhat* he consumed.

'Are you certain? You looked like you were in a lot of pain?'

He frowned. 'Sometimes it come painful, but not for such long time.' He looked away from me, his eyes distant and forlorn. 'I think it okay now!'

One minute Mani was doubled up with pain and then the next, as though nothing had ever happened, he was ready to set off again. I insisted he stay sitting for a while, to make certain he was better. I hadn't noticed him suffering any stomach pains until now, although I recalled when Akio tumbled over the path edge, Mani had seemed not quite himself.

A breeze descended on us as we sat in silence beneath the canopy of green. Mani continued to breathe cautiously while I stared blankly in the direction from which we had come and shivered. I was surprised to see how high we'd already climbed.

'I sometimes worry.' Mani's voice broke the silence.

'What about?' I replied.

'I think maybe I am unlucky,' he continued. That word again. 'When I am younger I have parents and sister. And sister, she has children too, I am uncle as well.' His voice wavered. 'Now all I have is sister's children, all the rest dead, they are all deaded.'

I was shocked. This had come out of nowhere. I remained silent to see if he had anything more to say, and when he hadn't I responded inadequately, 'That's terrible, all of them?'

'All of them!' The breeze seemed all that bit chillier as Mani spoke. 'First my parents, then my sister and then her husband. Now Mani give money for children so they not deaded too!'

This time Mani didn't try to mask his sadness with laughter. 'I think maybe I am unlucky!' His eyes welled up slightly as he rose to his feet. 'I think maybe I am very unlucky.'

There was nothing that I could say, it was too tragic a story that he had confided in me.

Mani seemed intent on starting off again; perhaps it was a useful distraction for him. Still, I was concerned.

'Are you sure you're ready to continue, Mani?' I watched him reaching for the backpack.

'No problem,' he patted his stomach optimistically, 'I think maybe just need *dal bhat*!'

He set off again and I followed closely behind.

Above the claustrophobic confines of the forest we came to a grassy clearing. 'We are up very high now,' explained Mani as he directed me to look over my shoulder. I turned around.

'My God, that is beautiful!' I scrambled for my camera. 'Do you see how amazing that looks?'

It was more than just open space; it was the scene of a lifetime. In every direction, the wonder and beauty of Nepal lay exposed, on show. I aimed my lens and snapped repeatedly. I couldn't control myself, it was like standing in a castle overlooking the world. Below was an artist's dream, each forest, each terraced patch of farmland, each snowcapped mountainside adding its own distinct hue. The wispy grey arms of a gentle mist only accentuated the beauty they tried to conceal.

Greatest of all were the towering protectors whose haunting forms tore patches from the blue morning sky: the Annapurna Mountains. As though they'd been watching us all along, they filled the sky behind with their enormous snow-capped presence, so massive yet still so far away.

Mani began to name the various peaks that were in view, leaving until last the Annapurna South peak whose base camp we were aiming to reach. For the minutes that we stood there taking everything in, I felt the most uplifted I'd been since as far back as I could remember.

I thought of home and the past. Just images. My mother's eyes first, honest and kind, ever hopeful; often she would look at me with those eyes as though she knew every thought that entered my head, and she'd make me feel safe.

I saw Dad's hands, coarse from a life on construction sites around the world, strong enough to keep on going, never to quit. Finally my brothers and sister, and the sounds of their youthful voices came to my ear, now long changed since the days when we played together, in the age before worries and disappointment. I pictured Sam, youngest of us all, and felt sad, knowing I hadn't spent enough time with him. He was a great brother, a gentle and unassuming guy now, who generally kept to himself. Even as kids he'd spent more time alone than he had with the rest of us.

I'll make a point of getting closer to him when I get home, I thought. Whenever I get home!

'You see,' said Mani, pointing down into the distance, 'there is Ghorepani!'

At least 400 metres below sat a tiny village.

'Why have all the houses got blue roofs?' At last I asked!

'They blue so that when we trek, we can see how far left to travel. You see, everything here is green, like trees, like forest. But nothing blue, easy for the eyes to see.' I should have figured that one out long ago! But Mani looked pleased to be sharing this with me.

'Easy here in Nepal!' he continued. 'We simple people!'

I smiled in agreement.

'Okay, we must continue, long way before first teahouse.' Mani turned to begin walking — but stopped, clutching once again at his stomach and letting out a low moan. Again I went to him. 'Okay?'

He threw a sharp, martyrish glance my way. 'No problem, just small pain, no problem.'

'Ghorepani is just down there. We can head back now and be there in no time.'

'No problem with me. I not want to go Ghorepani.'

'Well, let me carry the backpack then!' But this was utterly insulting to him.

'I am guide-porter. This is my job. I carry bag, you not to worry, I have no problem.' He spoke with disdain and I saw that I should back down. 'Okay. We go. Nearly two hours until first teahouse!' Mani gave an apologetic smile then, and set off again.

In the monotony of step after step after step, I cleared my mind of worry about stomach pain or Maoists, distracted by the veins that protruded from Mani's legs.

'You must not forget to give a small donation!'

I was in Varanasi, India, on the rooftop of the Golden Temple, surrounded by a labyrinth of dreary laneways interweaving weathered buildings, bleak and dark from lack of sunlight, stale from overcrowding. Below, on the ghat beside the Ganges, was a smouldering body. From the balcony edge I could see a large family grieving profusely as the body, draped in cloth but with the face visible, burnt upon a bed of chopped wood. It was an awful sight, too upsetting to watch. Those eyes that would never open, that face still fresh. It was a woman who looked little older than my mother.

I turned away from the sight.

'Donation for what?' I replied. The person who had spoken to me was a short Indian man, well dressed and confident in his manner.

'You see,' he gestured across the rooftop, 'this is a hospice! You know, place for the dying!'

People of all ages lay everywhere on the rooftop, sickly and awaiting death, their families close at hand, giving as much in the time that they had left to give. So much sorrow. So many people, and not one of them had caught my attention on the way in.

Someone grabbed hold of my hand. Startled, I spun around and looked into the smiling face of a young girl, her eyes sunken, face pale. Her body was thinner than I could ever have imagined. Repulsed, I tugged my hand away from her grip and hurried as fast as I could from the rooftop, stopping only to drop whatever coins I had in my pocket at the feet of an unknown form.

'Thank you.'

A moan from behind me acknowledged my coins as I sped down the stairs and out into the maze of streets.

My heart was thumping frantically and I felt ashamed and upset. The girl's innocent face lingered in my mind, and the depth of her sadness when I refused her hand. It was a terrible thing that I'd done.

Alone now and unnoticed in an empty laneway, I found myself leaning against a wall, tears falling from my eyes. What more heartache had I caused? Would I always be running away from something I'd done?

'Need a tissue?' The woman's voice was soft and warm. I looked up.

'I get like that sometimes too,' she continued lightly. 'It can be so upsetting to see, can't it?' She shook her head sympathetically.

I nodded and wiped my eyes, composing myself.

'India can bring anyone to tears! So, what's your name?'

'I'm Sean. What about you?' She seemed composed yet lively, with an impressive array of bright Indian jewellery. In the black fisherman's pants worn by seasoned travellers in India, she looked more suited to a stylish magazine than the streets of Varanasi.

'I'm Serena … You're Irish, aren't you?'

'And you're —' I paused for a moment, then took a stab in the dark — 'Australian?'

Her face lit up. 'Most people say American!'

Secretly pleased with my stroke of luck, I asked, 'How long have you been here for?'

'Well, I've been in Varanasi for two days, but I've been stuck in this maze of streets for the last three hours.'

I couldn't help but laugh.

'You're laughing now, but let's see you get us out of here,' she joked. 'Where are you going?'

'Wherever you want!' I took her hand and began to lead the way. She didn't let go, and we walked through the laneways, like sweethearts out for a stroll. There was an odd sense of comfort in walking hand in hand with this complete stranger.

'So how long have you been in India?' Serena asked.

'Only for a few weeks. I ran away from home!' What made me say that?

'Hanging out with a fugitive, am I?' Her easiness was infectious.

After a while she paused. 'Haven't we been down this street already! I'm nearly positive I've seen that cow before!'

A large spotted cow blocked our path and we edged our way around its backside, getting a slap from its tail as we passed.

'That's a different cow, it's a friend of the other one.'

'I still think we're lost,' she responded, giving me a mischievous grin.

'Trust me,' I said coyly. 'I have it all well under control. I'm bringing you the long way so that we can take in a bit of the scenery.' There was no scenery, nothing but narrow streets that were long ago forgotten by the sun.

'Are you here with anyone?' I asked in trepidation.

'Yeah. I'm here on my honeymoon!' A shiver ran down my spine but she squeezed my hand tightly. 'Only kidding. I'm here alone. I packed my bags, booked a ticket and here I am.'

We entered a street crowded with everything imaginable: people, cars, rickshaws, cattle; it was like trying to enter a football stadium while its last crowd was still leaving. I hung on to her tightly.

'Do you hear that?' she asked. 'Voices — chanting?'

It was low at first, just a hum growing in the distance, but definitely coming in our direction.

'What is it? A protest, a rally?'

'No,' she said. 'A funeral.'

And from around a corner there suddenly emerged a crowd — a hundred people, all running, and all chanting. Held aloft on a thin wooden bed was the draped body of an elderly woman, clearly on her way to the Golden Temple. Before we had time to comment, the crowd was passing by, a fleet of runners, their voices raised to the heavens.

'Come on. Follow the dead woman.' Serena released my hand. Together we ran among the swarm of mourners, behind their beloved departed, until finally the crowd reached the Golden Temple.

When I looked around, though, Serena was nowhere to be seen. She couldn't have gone too far, I thought, she had been right beside me.

I searched again. But she had vanished into thin air. As a last resort, I returned to the rooftop and looked down from the balcony for her. Still I couldn't see her — she had disappeared, just like that.

I turned for the exit and began to walk down the concrete stairs. Near the bottom I stopped, a sense coming over me that I was being watched. I turned, hoping to see Serena. She wasn't there; instead at the top of the stairs stood the young Indian girl whose hand I'd refused earlier.

'You look lost.' Her voice was soft and sweet, her big brown eyes looked at me without judgment, without any anger.

I gulped. Slowly I walked back up the stairs. The little girl watched. She seated herself on the top step and, on reaching it, I sat down beside her.

'I think perhaps I am a bit lost,' I replied. The young girl said nothing. 'What is your name?' I asked.

'My name is Bauna.' She played with her long black hair as she spoke. 'What is your name?'

'Mine's Sean.'

'That is very funny name!' She giggled and her face relaxed, releasing the carefree child from behind her sickly exterior. We sat in silence for a few moments.

'What is wrong with you?' I asked sympathetically.

'I am very sick,' she replied slowly. 'My mamma say soon I have to go far away —' She frowned. 'And I don't like to leave my mamma but she tell me she cannot come too!'

I placed my hand upon hers, and held it warmly for some time. She smiled happily.

Finally I stood up to leave.

'Do you want to see my mamma?' she asked excitedly.

'Ah, I better go,' I replied sadly. 'Maybe next time. It was lovely to meet you, Bauna, you're a very special young girl.' She smiled, bashful. 'You take care of yourself.'

I walked away from the Golden Temple, stopping once to wave goodbye to Bauna — but she too was gone.

8. *Hansel and Gretal*

'*Ahhh*!'

Quickly I ran to help Mani, as did a kind Nepalese man from a teahouse nearby. Tugging frantically at the backpack fasteners, I eased the load from Mani's shoulders while the elderly man questioned him in Nepali. Between quiet groans Mani answered.

'What's he telling you?' I asked the man. He didn't reply. Instead, he shook his head and led Mani towards his teahouse. Once there, he sternly instructed me to remain outside.

'I want to know what's going on,' I cried as the door was shut in my face. 'What is wrong with him?'

'He looks very sick.' I was startled. The words came from behind me and I turned. Instead of one face I met two — a man and a woman, both bronzed.

'Yeah, he does,' I replied. 'He's been having stomach ache all morning.'

'He sounded like he was in a lot of pain.' The girl spoke with concern, then pressed hard on her own stomach and mimicked the moan Mani had made. I found myself smiling at her; she had a comforting, naive simplicity.

'Maybe he's just had too much *dal bhat*,' I replied, and we all chuckled. 'I'm Sean, good to meet you.'

'I am Hans.'

'And I am Greta.'

'Ah, like Hansel and Gretal,' I said jokingly.

'No,' retorted Hans dryly, adding more slowly than before. 'My name is Hans and she is Greta.'

Hans was a tall, athletic-looking man with closely cut brown hair and a pair of rimless glasses. Greta was also very athletic looking, wearing a pair of loose khaki shorts and a light t-shirt. They resembled the adventure-seeking models that you would find in travel brochures or holiday documentaries.

'So, um, where are you trekking to?' I asked as a silence-filler.

'Oh, but of course we trek all over Nepal.'

Of course!

'We have been trekking already, forty-one days!' He

proceeded to recount each step of their forty-one-day hike as if reciting statistics. Greta remained silent, her eyes downcast, her hands playing with a stone that she must have picked up along the way. I couldn't help feeling that Greta didn't share Hans's enthusiasm for their journey. Hans continued to speak without leaving any opening for me to escape. Greta, on the other hand, found a dry place to sit, where she peeled off her boots and socks and began to massage her tired feet. They couldn't have appeared further apart if they had tried. I was becoming extremely bored by Hans's account.

'Are your feet sore?' I asked Greta, grabbing an opportunity to interrupt Hans as he paused for a breath. He shot me a look, unimpressed.

'She is fine,' he cut in. 'Girls, they are always complaining about their feet. Men are clearly the stronger sex.' Hans laughed, as Greta's face reddened with embarrassment.

'I think it is time we continue now.' Hans took a drink from his water flask, tucked it away and, without looking at Greta, heaved his backpack upon his shoulders and faced me once again. 'Nice to meet you, Sean. We travel the same way as you today, so maybe we meet in Tadapani tonight, yes?' He reached out and grabbed my hand. His grip was firm and his handshake strong and definite. Hans turned towards the trek path and started off again.

Without so much as a sharp word uttered, Greta and Hans had just had an argument in front of me, and now Hans was resorting to leaving without her. Within a matter of minutes he was out of view and Greta was petulantly tying her laces.

I felt I had to say something, as though I was at fault for asking after her feet.

'I'm sorry if I said the wrong thing to Hans!' Then I felt foolish to be apologising.

She glanced up at me with a wry smile.

'He always does this!' she mumbled angrily. 'I'm sick of everything he does, sick of it.' She pulled hard on the laces and finished the knot. I stood silently, watching, not sure what to say.

'Can I help? Do you want to talk about it?' I finally blurted.

A rush of emotion played over her face as she fought some inner demon. It was a battle lost. 'I'll tell you, forty-one days and tired.' She spoke with venom. 'Forty-one days and I hate this country and I ...' She paused for moment and then looked down at her clothing and began to tug at the jacket that was wrapped around her waist. 'And I hate this clothing and I … I hate him, I hate him!'

Oh. Maybe I'd said the wrong thing again. Probably should have minded my own business.

The resentment in her voice was intense. I wasn't sure what to do. Give her a hug or something? I made an awkward move towards her. She turned before I got close enough, distracted by her backpack, which she now threw angrily onto her shoulders.

'I'll tell you something else.' She faced me again, her fierce blue eyes staring hard into mine. 'I don't like walking!'

Then, planting an unexpected kiss on my cheek, she hurried off after her man and was soon gone. I was dumbstruck. Like an unexpected storm, the couple had arrived and left — sudden chaos, and then nothing! It was as though I'd imagined the whole thing.

The late morning sun had begun to settle in nicely over the countryside and the mist that had followed us for most of the morning's walk had finally drifted away. There was a sense of tranquillity here and I found my mind pleasantly at rest. The meeting with the German couple had distracted me from Mani — and now Mani heightened my contentment by emerging from the teahouse apparently revived.

'He give me medicine.' Mani patted his stomach and indicated his Nepalese helper. 'I think maybe it starting to work.'

'You feel better?' I was relieved.

'I feel good enough for *dal bhat*!'

I wasn't sure *dal bhat* was the remedy he was seeking. The elderly man attending him seemed to think the same thing and disappeared back into the house, his expression disapproving.

'He doesn't seem happy. What's wrong with him?' I asked Mani.

'He fine. He want Mani to rest but I think that maybe I feel good now!'

'Are you sure? If he thinks that you should rest maybe it's best to take his advice?'

'No.' Mani's smile retreated, almost becoming a frown. 'No, I now better. I am fine.'

Once again Mani had made his decision. And when the old man returned with menus and spoke pleasantly to Mani I felt a little more comfortable in his presence.

We remained at the teahouse for a further hour until Mani had finished eating. I argued with him one more time about carrying the bag, but he was adamant about it being his job, and I knew that if I persisted I would only be insulting him further rather than helping him.

As soon as we had left the village and were once again swallowed up by our trek, Mani led the way with renewed liveliness.

'I think it'll do you good,' I remember Mam saying to me as we arrived at the doctor's house. 'You're not getting on top of things. If anything, you're getting worse.'

At thirteen it was hard hearing those words. Mam was always my biggest supporter, and for her to say I was getting worse was like hearing that in her eyes I was a failure.

'I've started to get into music,' I pleaded. 'It makes me feel much better. Takes my mind off everything.'

But she wasn't convinced.

The doctor was young, probably not much older than thirty — I remembered thinking he was far too young to treat me.

In a lengthy discussion, I awkwardly recounted the many different things that I did, and then said what I thought my mind was doing.

'Sean,' he said, 'you suffer from an overactive imagination, which in your case adversely affects your Obsessive Compulsive Disorder — OCD.'

I had watched enough documentaries to know this already.

'What you probably don't know,' he continued, 'is that aside from prescribing medication — which, I might add, is something that I am never in favour of, except in the most severe of cases — your only way of dealing with this, probably, is to understand its mechanics.'

I became interested.

'Most anxieties come in a wave. People like you will feel a desire to do something, brought on by some kind of anxiety. In your case the anxiety can be, for example, that something will happen to your family if you don't perform a certain ritual. The trick is to not respond to the anxiety, but rather to let it follow its course. Anxiety starts small and like a wave will increase, becoming higher and higher. The thing to remember is that it will always decrease; it can't stay high forever. If you learn to ride the waves rather than get swallowed up by them, then you'll start controlling your OCD.'

That day I left the doctor's feeling invigorated and full of confidence. But it never worked! It never worked because life carries on, and the urge to perform a ritual is greater than allowing yourself to hold on and ride the wave.

*   *   *

Ahead, Mani was struggling up a steep incline.

'Do you want a break?' I cried out. An hour of hard walking had passed since we'd left the teahouse.

Mani didn't answer, simply nodded in an exhausted fashion and plonked himself down on a dry log of wood. We sat without saying a word for a short time. Finally Mani broke the silence.

'You know,' Mani nodded his head gently as he spoke, 'I was very worried!'

'About what?'

'My stomach! I tell you once all my family deaded, my sister, my mother, my father, everybody!'

How could I forget?

Mani continued, 'They all bleeded from their stomach, from their inside.'

'*All* of them?'

Mani's voice dropped to a lamenting whisper. 'Very sad for Mani, no family, all deaded.'

'But you feel much better now, don't you?'

'Now,' Mani spoke softly, his big eyes gleeful, 'yes, I am much better. Medicine working, I think.'

After a pause, Mani bowed his head. 'But still I am frightened whenever I am not feeling so well. Make me worry a lot. Make me think that maybe it is my time to be deaded too.'

The despair in Mani's voice moved me, though I was taken aback that he was telling me such personal details. What could I say to him?

'You're not going to die!' I tried, in a chirpy voice, 'Everybody gets stomach pains now and then. You're no different. It doesn't mean that we're all going to die, though. Only the other day I had a stomach ache myself. I was doubled up with pain.'

Mani looked at me, confused. 'Doubled … up… What is this?'

'It means … really bad pain.'

'Ah,' his voice rose. 'Really bad, I understand.' He mulled over this for a second. 'So you, too, had pain in your stomach?'

'Yeah, terrible — turned out I had a serious case of gas!'

'Gas?' Again he was confused.

'Yeah, you know, I needed to let out a massive fart, and then I was cured!' Animatedly, I demonstrated what I meant and could tell that Mani understood by the bashful look on his face. But his bashfulness was quickly replaced by worry once again. Mani was frightened. Too many hours with your own thoughts can be hazardous. I knew.

'You see,' he continued, 'maybe stomach pain okay for you, but here in Nepal, sickness sometimes very bad, even small sickness many time kill. For a man like me, guide-porter, not always long life, not so much money for medicine.' He broke off suddenly, collecting his thoughts. 'I want to find wife, I want to make good life for my family, I not want to be deaded.'

Where was the window that I could climb out of? I didn't think I was the right person for this job. Still, sometimes it's best to tell people what they want to hear, even if you know it mightn't be entirely true. Mani needed something to raise his spirits not sadden him further.

'Didn't you say that the medicine is making you feel better?' Mani nodded. 'And the rest of your body is feeling okay? No other pains?' He nodded again. 'Well, then maybe you've nothing to worry about at all, you've nothing but a stomach bug.'

'Bug?'

'Yes,' I continued. 'A bug in your stomach. One that'll soon go away.'

Mani stared at me inquiringly, his brain slowly deciding whether or not to believe me. 'You sure?'

'I promise you!'

He looked relieved. Was I right to make promises about things I couldn't control?

'Maybe you are right. I think Mani still alive for time much more.'

I returned this optimism with a gentle nod.

'But,' he became serious again, 'if I stay living, I not want to live here in Nepal. Life no good here.'

This had surfaced out of nowhere.

'I have some friend in Israel and she say I can go there. I want to do that.' Then, slyly looking in my direction, he added, 'And in your country, maybe I can get job there too, maybe you help Mani also?'

My jaw almost dropped. Where was this discussion going? Had Mani just pulled a fast one on me — a sales pitch through sympathy? This had happened before in my travels.

But I tried not to show annoyance, unwilling as yet to rule Mani out so fast.

'When I try to go to Israel I write letter to my friend for sponsor. She send me letter that say she will give me job and house and she will help me in Israel.' He opened his wallet and drew out a piece of paper, neatly folded, from one of the pouches. We looked at it together. The letter had been written to the Nepali immigration office.

'So what did you do?' I asked, handing it back to him.

'I think maybe I am unlucky. I go to immigration with letter and ask if I can leave. They say no. They say I have to pay two hundred lakh as present to immigration manager.'

'As a present!' I exclaimed. 'As a bribe, more like it.' Two hundred lakh — two hundred thousand rupees — was more money than Mani could save in a lifetime. But bribery was normal in Nepal. And immigration officers believed that if a Nepalese can afford to leave the country, then they must be very wealthy and should share some of that wealth around. As Mani talked about it, I realised I'd never met a Nepalese outside Nepal, in all of my years of travelling.

It was a beautiful country but poor. Who wouldn't want to try for something better elsewhere? Mani was just a man trying to make good — an honest guide who struggled from one week to the next to make a living. If I could give him some ray of hope what did it hurt me?

After a few minutes of riffling through my backpack, I found a scrap of paper and a pen.

'There you go,' I said after I'd written on the paper. 'That's my address in Ireland, and my phone number.

When this trek is over and I've gone back home — maybe in three months, I made a wild guess — you contact me and I'll see what I can do for you, okay?'

Appalling as his situation was, giving him my address, I knew, was more of an easy gesture than a real promise — like throwing a few coins and then walking on by.

The familiar blue rooftops indicating Tadapani looked dull under the overcast sky but were still a welcome sight.

'It looks quite near.' From where we stood, the town looked about forty-five minutes' walk away.

'Two hours.' He pointed. 'We go down first, and then all the way back up.'

I shook my head. So close, yet so far away! The network of forest was so dense that there was no definition of contours; the lower levels of the valley were indistinguishable, camouflaged. I imagined a huge bridge across the valley. That would save some steps!

We started off once again, a light drizzle now encouraging the leeches to emerge. They seemed to sneak up on you when you least expected it. Walking along you'd suddenly feel a slight tingle at a point on your body and on investigation you were guaranteed to find one — generally stuck tight to your skin with one end buried deep into your flesh, sucking blood relentlessly. They never seemed to bother Mani though; then again they hardly went near him. I too had been quite lucky but with the arrival of rain it was becoming clear that leeches had a fondness for Irish blood.

But as much as leeches made things difficult, the drizzle was also quite pleasant — like the gentle rain, back home in Ireland.

I thought about sitting in the living room looking out the window one day when I was about sixteen, gazing into the backyard. It was midday, but it could as easily have been close to nightfall, the way the cloud cover had extinguished the sun's light. Rain was gently tip-tapping on the window.

'What a terrible day,' Dad suddenly said as he entered the room.

I looked up, embarrassed to see him. 'I don't think we've had a summer this year,' I said.

Dad had the newspaper in his hand. He sat down on the couch close to me and we were silent for the next few minutes.

Eventually I said, 'Sorry about last night!'

Dad had been waiting for me to say it all day and perhaps that was why he had come into the room. The previous night he had caught me mid-ritual. I hadn't noticed him come into my room because I had my eyes closed — but when I opened them I was paralysed by the expression on his face.

'Do you do this often?' he'd said, dismayed.

I had been trying desperately to complete a prayer for about ten minutes. Had Dad witnessed it all?

'No!' I became angry and defensive.

'So what's going on then? You've been standing there for ages doing the same thing over and over again! Talk to me — tell me what this is all about! Is this another outbreak of your OCD?'

Dad was always such a caring father, but on that day I wasn't having it.

'Forget it, Dad, there's nothing wrong. Mind your own business. Just mind your own business!' And I'd stormed out like a spoilt kid. So here he was, acknowledging my apology with a gentle grin and presumably still wondering what madness possessed his son. But he said nothing. I had hurt him, I knew.

After about forty-five minutes' walking we reached the centre of the valley. 'It's beautiful here,' I exclaimed.

A gentle stream meandered slowly beneath a broken old bridge and all around towered trees of every shape and size. Under their canopy, it was as though we'd entered a forgotten place; deathly still but, in a strange way, peaceful.

'Phew, we got down here fast enough,' I gasped, trying to catch my breath.

'But now come the hard part.' Mani pointed a finger towards the track, which began again on the other side of the bridge. It was dramatically steep. Before long both of us were reduced to an uninspired pace. With that came the monotony. Then, as always, came the thoughts.

I bet they're really pissed off.

Frustrated by this guilt creeping up on me again, I shook my head, hoping that the thought would subside and crawl back to where it had come from. It didn't.

Up and leaving like that, without any reason. They must have been worried sick.

I fought back, rubbing my fingers abrasively over each other, getting horribly upset.

I've told you, I'm not thinking about this. There was nothing else for me to do at the time. If I stayed, God knows what could have happened!

I paused and then continued, vexed.

No, that's a load of crap. Nothing would ever have happened. I would have done myself in before hurting anyone else. I'm not talking about this bullshit any more. I called home when I was in India and everyone's cool, they understand.

I tried to distract myself by concentrating on each step on the muddy trail. The rain that had threatened since we set off had increased from drizzle to a light shower and the cool evening air was settling in fast. Even though I was sweating from the climb, the rainfall was icy and I was shivering as I walked. But we'd advanced about halfway up the incline already. That's when we heard the roar.

'Where did that come from?' I whispered, catching up with Mani's stock-still form. A second roar echoed in the distance and both of us swung around.

'Over there!' Mani pointed fearfully towards the opposite side of the steep valley which we had just ascended. 'Very hard to see.'

There was just a wallpaper of trees. Suddenly a slight movement caught my eye. It was in a clearing about twenty minutes' walk behind us.

'It's ...' Mani squinted into the distance. 'It's Akio!' He instantly became alarmed. 'Can you see? It's Akio.'

'No way — is it?' My heart began to thump as I tried to identify the figure standing in the centre of the clearing. It was a man alright, but he had his back to me. 'Turn around,' I cried. 'Let me see who you are.'

'We should stay quiet,' warned Mani.

But as though he'd heard, the man turned suddenly, erratically; it *was* Akio. Instinctively I leapt out of view, concealing myself behind a tree, avoiding the gaze which Akio fixed in our direction.

'Oh shit,' I whispered. 'He's in danger.' Clearly Akio was in trouble, he didn't even have his backpack any longer.

'Must be the Maoist,' replied Mani. 'I think we must go away from here. I think we go fast!'

Mani couldn't conceal his fear, but now I couldn't hide my curiosity. Crawling to an area of greater cover I gazed down once more, watching Akio's every movement. He'd started running again, his small form barely visible as it zigzagged in and out of clearings and down the mountainside.

'Come, Sean!' Mani tugged hard on my arm. 'We must go. We stay and maybe Maoist come for us too.'

These words jolted me into action. The Maoists were the last people that I wanted to meet again.

Mani led the way — much faster than in all the time I'd known him. The track was slippery, wet and forever uphill. We powered on as if we had all the energy in the world and only a short time to use it. Every few metres I would look back, partly out of worry for myself, but mainly out of concern for Akio.

The stupid idiot, I thought, walking frantically. He just couldn't keep his mouth shut and give them some fucking money. Selfish bastard! He'd made life difficult for everybody.

I began to drop back a little from Mani. Suddenly we entered another clearing and I was compelled to stop for another look. At first there was nothing to see. Then, from out of nowhere, three people dashed into view and back into the depths of the forest. They were moving fast and weren't too far behind us.

Please Holy God, please protect Mam, Dad …

I began reciting aloud, the words running from my mouth on their own as I searched for another glimpse of Akio.

… and please protect Mani and me and —

Akio's name came into my mind, a clawing requirement to include him or the prayer wouldn't be correct and therefore he'd be in even greater danger than he already faced. I was angry with him, though. I had to include him but I didn't want to; my praying couldn't help him, he'd brought this on himself.

How could you possibly wish him harm? If something happens to him it's all your fault. Dear Holy God ...

I tried to push the hostility to the back of my mind, then suddenly Akio appeared again and I was distracted from the prayer without Akio's name being successfully included.

He had come out into a patch of open space through which I could see the bridge we'd passed over earlier. He looked confused and frightened. It seemed as though he was deciding what to do next, where to run or where to hide — but he was deciding too slowly. From behind him, the three men emerged into view. A barrage of frantic prayers bludgeoned my mind. I wanted to yell out to Akio — *Run!* But no words left my mouth. My mind was too occupied to release my tongue for anything other than prayers.

Mani shouted at me, '*Come*, Sean, you must hurry, you in big danger.'

His words startled me, broke me away from my thoughts. I didn't move though, I was glued to the spot. What was taking place in the valley a little way below was too terrifying detach myself from.

The three men circled Akio, each brandishing weapons, each poised and moving aggressively. The first blow landed hard across Akio's face, throwing him almost weightlessly to the ground. I was too far away to see for certain, but something made me think that the first to deliver a punch was Raja.

Akio began to scramble to his feet, his hands pressed hard against his bloody face, his body looking weak and vulnerable.

Dear Holy God, please protect … dear Holy God please protect Mam, Dad … dear Holy God … Say Akio, say Akio … Get it right!

I started over and over again. New additions always had to be placed at the end of the prayer — but since I wasn't getting that far without having to start again, each new start was becoming more frantic, more desperate, and I still hadn't included Akio.

A swift hard kick from one of the other men toppled again with ease. His body squirmed. Clearly he was in excruciating pain.

Dear Holy God.

I started reciting loudly, closing my eyes tightly, eliminating any distractions, anything that might prevent me from completing the prayer and helping Akio!

'Come!'

I leapt back startled again. Mani had returned to get me.

'They're going to kill Akio!' I pointed to the clearing below. 'Shit! Where has he gone?' I scanned in every direction. 'They've all disappeared, where are they?'

'Come, we must run. I think maybe soon *bang bang*!'

Just as Mani finished speaking there was a loud blast, swiftly followed by two more.

'Gunshots?' I cried.

Mani nodded.

'For Godsake! Do you think he's dead?'

'I think so,' he replied. 'Maybe! We must run, I think they looking for us too!'

Panic-driven, I jumped once again to my feet. My hands were shaking feverishly and for a moment I didn't know what to do. Mani grabbed hold of me and once again dragged me in the direction of Tadapani village.

The next hour followed in a blur of fear, exhaustion, confusion and anxiety. Each step no longer felt like agony, it felt like escape, with no option of turning back. Mani walked rapidly, flushed red, the sound of his heavy breathing accompanying each impatient step. He looked more like a machine than a man hauling a backpack on his shoulders.

I pounded behind in a daze. Still none of the prayers were reaching completion and my mind told me that I was to blame for what had happened to Akio. I knew it was ridiculous to be thinking like that but, as always, the grinding guilt outweighed any form of rational thinking.

Dear Holy God ... Fuck! It's my fault, it's my fault.

'Tadapani,' Mani gasped as he pointed up ahead.

It was like somebody had just turned on the light in an otherwise darkened room and suddenly everything became clear again. We were close to collapse, but seeing Tadapani lifted our spirits and we focused on reaching the end. As we surfaced from the confines of the forest into the open space of the village, the rain fell more heavily than it had all afternoon.

Finally we reached the sheltered decking of the Everest Lodge. Mani threw the backpack to one side and himself alongside it. Lying flat on his back, he struggled to catch his breath, until at last his panting settled to a steady wheeze. I remained standing for a short while, reminded of gym, at school, where we were always told it was best to calm your breathing while still standing — a strange way to be thinking after the ordeal of the day. Finally I stretched out beside Mani.

'How are you feeling?' I mumbled at last.

Mani remained silent for a while, his mind some place else. Finally he answered, 'Mani not so bad, tired I think. Sad also.'

'I can't believe what happened to Akio. It was —'

Mani interrupted me. 'Tonight we eat and then sleep, not stay awake for long. Maoist might come here tonight, safer for us to sleep, maybe Maoist not see us.'

Poor Mani. He was pale in the face, he was worried and he was sick. And I worried for his livelihood. Would the Maoists hold him responsible? Would he be able to take future treks through this country?

'Do you think Akio *is* dead?'

'If he has luck like Mani, yes!'

He rose to his feet and disappeared through a door at the end of the creaky decking. I remained alone, deep in my thoughts, surprisingly comforted now by the sound of the rainfall.

Dear Holy God …

I spoke slowly, aloud, pronouncing each word precisely and with definition.

… please protect Mam, Dad, John, Sarah and Sam, Benji and Rusty, all my friends and relatives, Mani and …

I couldn't do it.

'Shit!' I roared aloud in anger. 'Damn you, Akio. Damn, damn, damn. *Akio* is your name, *Akio*. How hard is that to say? Holy God, if Akio's not dead, look after him for fucksake and while you're doing it, give me a fucking break.'

I couldn't contain my anger. If my emotion had had a physical form, I would have drawn it out and punched it there and then. But I couldn't. And no sooner had the words parted from my lips than came the guilt.

Maybe I shouldn't have said that. If Akio is still alive I've probably just ruined any chance he has left.

Dear Holy God, sorry about that, sorry for cursing, please protect …

It was no use and I was too exhausted. I closed my eyes and concentrated only on the sound of the rainfall. From out on the street it sounded like a continuous hum; from somewhere nearby the lodge it sounded like a beat, tapping gently on some steely surface; and from behind it was a single drop every three seconds or so. Above, the trees rocked in the wind, and in the distance the gush of a river could be heard.

Without noticing, I drifted off to sleep.

9. *A bump in the night*

'Okay, wake-up time, no sleeping here.'

My eyes opened and I left behind what had seemed to be a perfect sleep. It was nightfall and Mani was standing over me, dangling a room key. I wondered who might have seen me sleeping out here on the open deck.

'You are room number three. There is no water and no *electric*. It is better that we eat and then sleep right after.'

I followed Mani to the end of the decking where a door led to the dining area. This was a dark room, uncomfortably cold, where a few scattered candles flickered dimly. A stubble-faced teenage boy emerged from an area unknown and, after I ordered, vanished again.

The bleakness of the restaurant was heightened by the shadows that were cast across the walls; I could have sworn I saw Akio's face among the many different shapes that danced there.

Dear Holy God …

My praying hadn't stopped; the horror of what had happened was only starting to set in.

He must be dead. The poor guy! I just can't believe it. This isn't the holiday I planned. I never signed up for this.

What if the Maoists are still trying to find me.

The food soon arrived, set down by a very pregnant woman who breathed heavily as she moved. She didn't engage in conversation and I was once again left alone to my thoughts.

Why would the Maoists be bothered with me? I had paid the stupid donation, I had done what they wanted. I spooned the *dal bhat* into my mouth and remembered punching Raja. Did he hold a grudge? The food slid down my throat in a thick uncooked lump. It was tasteless and cold. I'd meant to hit him, to get things back into some kind of order. He was going to kill Akio —

I frowned. Well, maybe he did!

Dear Holy God — I wish I was home!

As raw and unpleasant as my dinner was, I ate it all. There was nothing else to do in this room, and I was resigned to having an early night. I *wanted* an early night. What is it: fight or flight? I wanted to curl up and let this nightmare pass right by.

Reluctantly I rose up from the table and went outside to the deck. It was darker now and raining, and the boards creaked under my feet. At room number three I fumbled with the key. It was hard to see and I became increasingly jumpy. Finally the key drove into the lock and the door quickly flung open, startling me. I darted defensively in every direction — but there was nothing there. Uneasily, I entered, unable to shake the feeling that I was being watched as I'd headed for the room.

Shutting the bedroom door, I threw myself down upon the wafer-thin mattress with a thud. I don't know why I expected the bed to be softer. I closed my eyes tightly. Best to keep them closed.

'You awake?' Serena's voice. It was the early hours of the morning and moments earlier she had been fast asleep by my side. The fan in our Goan beach hut purred above and in the distance the sea washed into shore in a constant rhythm.

'Yes,' I replied, wondering what had woken her.

'Why?' she whispered. 'Are you worried?'

'I can't click off,' I replied. 'And the darkness of this room is playing tricks with my head.'

Serena put her arm around me and nestled closely alongside.

'Okay,' she said sleepily, 'let's make a deal. We're not allowed to think of anything or say anything for the next five minutes. Not one thing. Deal?'

I thought for a second. 'Deal.' I cleared my mind of all thoughts and worries. I don't think I lasted more than one minute.

I went unconscious.

Think of nothing. Don't think about Akio, don't think about Ireland. Think of nothing. Here we go!

How long was I asleep? I didn't know but a gentle knock on the door disturbed me. Had I dreamt it?

The knock sounded again. I was instantly petrified. *Who the hell was this?*

I tiptoed towards the door keeping deathly silent. As I reached it I suddenly had a change of plan and returned to my backpack. Searching quietly through its contents I found myself a weapon. My trusty torch.

The knocking became louder but I maintained my silence.

'Open the door. It's me.' The voice was soft and familiar. Easing my grasp on the torch, I opened the door.

'Can I come in?' She spoke in a whisper and by her shivering I could see that she'd been knocking for some time.

'Greta! Come in.' I switched on the torch. 'What are you doing here? Are you alright?'

'I'm fine, a little cold. I saw you tonight as you were leaving for your room. I hope you don't mind me being here?'

She was wearing nothing but an unzipped jacket and a light shirt, probably belonging to Hans. The shirt was only partially buttoned — open enough to reveal a hint of cleavage and short enough to show her shapely legs up to where her white knickers began. She looked beautiful — and freezing.

'Of course not,' I said. 'Come in and sit down.' I pointed towards the bed and she folded herself into a cross-legged position upon the mattress. I diverted my eyes for a minute, to allow her the privacy to adjust her position. But she remained in the same posture, and secretly I was pleased.

'So, when did you get here?' I asked as a distraction. 'I never saw you guys along the track!'

'Hans got here at about two o' clock. I arrived some time after three!'

Oh shit. I had temporarily forgotten about Hans. 'So where is Hans now?' The words left my tongue guiltily.

She frowned as she spoke. 'He is in our room, sleeping. Don't worry, he doesn't know that I'm here. I don't think that he would care.'

A sigh of relief escaped from my mouth. Much as I tried not to look, Greta's crossed legs seemed to capture my gaze. I looked away again.

'So, what can I do for you?' It sounded sleazier than I'd intended. 'I mean what can I help you with?'

Don't be a scum bag, she's got a boyfriend for Godsake.

She looked at me uneasily for a moment, then, in a tone of authority, announced, 'Firstly, no sex!' The sentence was like a blow.

'We cannot have sex because —' she pressed her forefinger to her the crotch of her knickers — 'she is on holiday for a few days.' Greta's frankness was incredible. 'Secondly, I only want to sleep. I want Hans to learn a lesson. When he comes looking for me and finds me lying in your arms he will know that he must treat me better in the future.'

Silence followed, as I tried to collect my thoughts.

'No sex!'

On reflection, it wasn't the best thing to say first, especially since I was just as shocked by everything else that she was suggesting. Still, in situations like that, who could ever predict what might tumble from your mouth? I became flustered — a mixture of amusement and embarrassment.

Greta looked at me with dismay. 'You men are all the same. You're only interested in sex, nothing else. You want to come inside of me and that is it!'

Again, that was forthright!

'Wait a minute there,' I said, regaining control. 'Now, firstly, I don't want to have sex with you.' I had to look slightly to the left of her to make that sound convincing. 'And secondly —' I was in full attack — 'what are you playing at anyway?'

Greta wasn't fazed. After some reflection, she began again, this time with a change in tone. She spoke slowly, her lips pouted, her hand gestures becoming more alluring as she talked.

'All I want is your help, the help from a friend. Maybe we can have sex too, maybe.' Greta eased herself from her sitting position and, on hands and knees, crawled across the mattress towards me. 'Won't you help me, Sean?' As she crawled, her shirt shifted its position on her body, revealing her naked breasts and her pert behind.

This doesn't feel right!

'Wait a minute.' I stepped off from the bed and backed away, regaining some sense as I retreated.

'What is it?' she purred. 'Simple deal, I do something for you and you do something for me!'

Simple deal maybe, but I'm damned if I'm going to be the idiot. I don't care if you're hot as hell.

'Greta,' I opened the door, exposing the room to the cold night air, 'you've got to go!'

'But Sean, what's the problem?'

'What's the problem?' Oddly, I was surprised. 'I'll tell you what the problem is. You're the problem. You and Hans! I'm not getting involved in your screwed-up relationship. God knows I have enough problems of my own without taking on yours as well!'

'But there's no problem. Hans isn't going to fight with you if that's what you're worried about.'

'That's not what I'm worried about, I just ...' I thought and then continued calmly, 'Greta, to put it vulgarly, I don't want to add another screw to a relationship that's already rightly screwed as it is. Now you've got to go, you've got to leave.'

She stared at me. She was scheming something again, but I wasn't sure what.

'I'm not going to go.' Greta lay down upon the bed, opening her legs as she spoke. 'I'm not going until Hans comes to get me.' She began to undo her top and, on some other occasion, I would have jumped her then and there. She was smug and sexy, but I was fed up. Lunging towards her and grasping one of her ankles, I dragged her, kicking, until she was within inches of falling off the bed.

'You are going.' I grabbed her by the wrist and thrust her gently towards the door.

She looked back. 'But Sean.'

'No buts.' I pushed her by the shoulders out the door. 'Goodnight, Greta,' I said, as I released my hold. With a light tap on her arse, I closed the door firmly behind her.

10. The race

Akio ... probably dead ... Dear Holy God please protect ... Dear Holy God ...

'Shut up, it's too early,' I moaned.

It was a bitterly cold morning. The thoughts were flowing whether I wanted them to or not, though I was still half asleep. I began reciting, prayer after prayer, struggling to dress.

As I went out along the cold open decking it was still raining, though the heavy falls of the night had reduced to a misty drizzle. The light was quite bright too, so perhaps there'd be sunshine later on.

Six successful prayers!

Ordinarily I'd be lucky to get one to work. It was no use, though — on that morning I needed to do seven correctly, not six, otherwise all of them would be wrong. It infuriated me, but there was no choice. I started the seventh.

Although once would usually suffice, there were extremes when seven was the number I'd have to aim for — to know things were done properly. Seven prayers in a row, seven times hand-washing, seven times reciting somebody's name. It drove me up the wall.

Dear Holy God please protect Mam, Dad … Shit!

There was a sudden stabbing pain. I looked down. Four leeches were tucking into my foot.

The bastards. Now I'd screwed up the last prayer and would have to start all seven again.

'I'm sick of all this bullshit!' I flung the leeches away and began praying again, openly out on the open deck.

At full speed I recited each prayer — fast enough to prevent any sabotaging distractions from entering my head. With fingers and toes tensed, in an upright position on my heels, and my eyes fastened tight, finally prayer seven ended successfully.

Thank God!

'Coming for breakfast?'

His voice surprised me as I emerged from the toilet.

'Hans!' I said, guardedly. 'You're up early!'

'Of course. It is always best to start as soon as the sun rises.'

Of course!

Hans seemed to be cheerful enough, though. He recounted the previous day's trek like a drill sergeant — emotionless and methodical.

When we entered the eating hall, Greta was already there, sitting at the head of the single wooden table. She was sipping on a hot drink, and looked distantly out the window.

'Good morning, Greta,' I said, to see how she would react.

'Ah, Sean, how are you today?'

'I'm okay.' She gave nothing away. 'Hans said you guys got here before me yesterday?'

She nodded her head nonchalantly and returned her attention to the view on the other side of the windowpane.

We ordered breakfast and then distanced ourselves by withdrawing into our own private thoughts. Hans occasionally made comments regarding the day's journey. I mulled over whether or not to continue with the trek. Despite reaching Tadapani, I was still fearful about what lay ahead. My hands were trembling as I lifted my cup of warm tea to my mouth.

But Tadapani was in the middle of nowhere: there was no easy way back to Pokhara except through our next stop, Chomrung. I certainly didn't want to go back to Ghorepani. I frowned.

Akio wasn't the only reason to cut the trek short; my own mental state was beginning to really worry me. There was too much time to think; each day's trek only meant hours of private time, which was not a good thing for a guy like me.

As I sat eating my breakfast I automatically rubbed one foot over the surface of the other. Catching myself doing this, I blanched. *What are you doing?*

It had been years since I'd practised the foot-rubbing ritual. It was a simple thing that had first sparked it off. One day, while playing football with my younger brother in the backyard, an idea had sprung into my mind — if my brother should happen to come into contact with my foot, something bad would happen to him. Then, while tackling me, he did touch my foot. I brushed off the consequences. It was just a stupid thought that I'd had and nothing more.

Later that afternoon though, Sam was riding his bicycle and had an accident. He came down hard off a kerb and bit into his tongue, almost severing it into two.

Sam recovered. I was the one who got sick. I immediately convinced myself that it was entirely my fault. If I hadn't mentally connected Sam's wellbeing with touching my foot he would never have come off his bike. Now I knew I had to develop a safeguard. Any similar thoughts I might have in future would have the same effect. From then on, if I had any premonitory feelings, I would rub one foot over the other. If I thought someone was going to be sick, I would do it. If I thought about a car crash, I would do it. Anything. It was a ridiculous ritual and I knew it. Somehow it had faded — but no ritual was ever really dead.

Discovering that morning in Nepal years later that I was rubbing one foot over the other, especially in the company of Hans and Greta, came as a horrible shock. Immediately I stopped.

'You are not a decent man.' Hans spoke to me with complete contempt.

'I'm not — what?' What was he on about?

'So far this morning I have been friendly with you. I am not a violent man. But —' he paused for effect — 'I thought that by now you would have apologised!'

'Apologise? For what? I didn't do anything.'

Greta was still distracted by her window.

'You see my girlfriend?' Greta turned to face Hans, her manner sulky and cold.

'Yeah, what about her?'

'She told me that last night you tried to sleep with her.'

'She told you what?' My voice rose an octave in surprise. 'That's bullshit.'

I looked at Greta, who remained cool and composed. 'Greta, tell him the truth.'

Both Hans and I gazed at Greta, waiting for her side of the story.

Softly she began to speak, her eyes darting longingly at Hans. 'It is true. Last night before I came to bed, Sean met me outside of his room.' She looked away. 'He began to touch me and then asked me if I wanted to sleep with him.'

'That's a load of crap,' I exploded.

Hans was confused. He looked at Greta and then at me, searching for the truth. As he turned from her, Greta lifted her head secretively and threw a gentle smile my direction. It wasn't devious; it was honest and I knew what she meant by it. Then she lowered her head once again.

'Okay!' I raised my open hands. 'You got me, I'm sorry.'

Hans turned quickly. 'Huh-ha!' He pointed a finger at me. 'So you did try to sleep with her!'

'Who wouldn't? Greta's a beautiful woman.' I looked directly at her. 'I'm sure guys try to crack on to her all the time.'

Hans thought for a moment. Would he want to beat the shit out of me? No. Greta had been right, it wasn't his way to fight. With an explanation, he was happy.

'I suppose you are right. Greta is very beautiful and you are not the first and will not be the last. I can see why you might try to sleep with her!'

This sounded strangely like a man talking about his prized hunting dog. Greta slid over beside Hans and kissed him on the cheek, grabbing hold of his hand.

'Come on, Hans, let's go. I don't want to stay in here with him.'

Hans and Greta headed for the door, neither of them looking back, and soon I was alone, feeling unjustly condemned but amused. I smiled to myself. But before I could get too comfortable, the door opened again and Greta came rushing back.

'I told him that I forgot my diary!' She pulled it out from underneath her jacket and smiled at me slyly. 'Oops.'

Then she leant over and pressed her lips upon mine. As the kiss developed I was impressed.

'Not bad,' Greta said in approval, as she broke away and stared at me seductively. 'Maybe next time, we can do more than this. Thank you!'

She swiftly turned on her heels and within seconds disappeared out of the room. All I could do was laugh, and it felt damn good.

What a girl! God help poor old Hans.

An hour later there was still no sign of Mani in the eating hall. With nobody around, I was easily managing the prayers and rituals that needed to be done before we left. Seven times each now — without seeing any of my own reflections or shadows around the room. Whenever I was drained or tired, if my reflection or shadow happened to come into view during a prayer it meant that I was praying to myself instead of to God, and therefore the prayer wouldn't work. I'd have to start again. Very little daylight was entering this room and there were no mirrors anywhere.

Just as I completed all the rituals, the door opened and there was Mani.

'We better go.' He looked pale and weak. And anxious.

'But you haven't eaten yet.'

'Today Mani not need food, we must go.'

'Not even *dal bhat*?' I persisted.

'Not even *dal bhat*!'

I had visions of three Maoist men outside, waiting for us with their guns loaded and at the ready, but aware of Mani's stomach troubles I hesitated.

'Time we leave!' he commanded.

There was awkwardness in the room. Just as before, Mani didn't want to discuss whatever was wrong. Still, I had to ask him. 'Are you feeling okay? — You look very pale!'

'Pale?' Mani's bloodshot eyes lit up in inexplicable fury. 'Mani not look pale, you look pale! No problem with me, Mani fine!'

I was quite surprised. It was the first time I'd seen Mani angry. Then I felt responsible — I'd probably driven him to it.

'Sorry, I was only joking. I'll go put on my gear.'

Hurriedly I dressed myself in the wet trekking gear back in my room.

Mani was waiting for me on the sheltered decking outside. Only ten minutes had passed but he seemed different, his mood transformed. Grinning happily, he took the backpack from my hands and strapped it to his shoulders.

'I get more medicine,' he told me cheerfully then. 'Woman in house give to me, already I feel better.' He patted his stomach.

'Ah!' I said. 'So that's why you were so grumpy earlier. Are you sure you don't want to rest for longer?'

'No, I think no problem. I think that maybe I am unlucky, but medicine bring me good luck!'

Mani stepped out from beneath the shelter into the light rain, and I followed obediently. We were on our way again.

The first half of the day's journey passed quickly. The downpour became heavier — so heavy that we just moved as briskly as possible. So much for sunshine.

The track was mostly uphill but given how frantically we'd walked the previous evening it felt easy. Akio and the Maoists occasionally came into my mind, but for the most part the terrain was too rough and the rainfall too heavy to allow me to brood: too many dangers and no room for distractions.

After about four hours, we reached our lunch stop, just as the rain subsided. The clouds parted enough to treat us to our first taste of sunlight that day and the wind eased up. We entered the only teahouse and the table and chairs were a welcome sight.

Mani seemed decidedly cheery, and he sat with me for lunch. 'In your country, are there jobs for guide or porter?'

As always, his questions arrived out of nowhere. 'Not really.' I wanted to break it to him nicely. 'The countryside hasn't as many mountains as here.'

'No mountains?'

'Well, there are mountains but just not a lot of them. Mostly, it's very flat.' I pressed my hand upon the table to demonstrate.

'Ah, very flat, I understand.' He frowned. 'So if I come to your country, will there be work for me? Maybe I would like to clean, is there work for cleaning?'

'Of course, there's loads of cleaning jobs.' His spirits lifted once again and I continued. 'In Ireland there are many big factories and they always need cleaners, hard workers, anyone who is not frightened to get their hands dirty.'

'Get hands dirty?'

'Yeah, you know, work very hard!' Mani understood what I meant, and I could see that it gave him hope. He raised his hands and showed them to me.

'Already dirt!' he said with a smile.

'Mine too.' I returned the display.

'And in Ireland,' he continued, 'do many people do the same like you?' Mani began to rub his hands together to demonstrate what he meant.

At first I didn't know what to say. He'd thrown me. When had he seen me? But I was being foolish. I knew what a slave to them I'd become!

'Oh that …' I began awkwardly. 'That's not very Irish, that's just me!'

'Why you do that?' Mani's eyes were intense and curious.

'Because when I am very bored, it makes time pass faster for me.' How lame.

'I don't think so.' Mani spoke suddenly, and instantly I felt defensive.

'It's true. I'm not lying.'

Silence fell on us both, and I hoped it would remain. But no.

'I think that maybe, like I am not so lucky, you are not so happy!'

'I'm happy!' I began to fight in my corner. 'I'm very happy. Who wouldn't be happy, especially being in such a beautiful place like Nepal? This is the happiest I've been in years.'

Mani wasn't convinced. I wasn't convincing myself either.

'When I am happy I want to stay happy. Sometimes life is too short.' Mani spoke wistfully. 'If you are so happy then why lose so much time with your eyes closed and so in pain with your head?'

I ate the rest of my lunch in silence, a silence that Mani respected. If I could have found a hole in the ground to bury my embarrassed face in, I'm sure I would have done it. It was frightening to be discovered for who you really are.

We nearly all live our lives in some kind of disguise. Some people make it their life's mission to be open and honest about who they are, to reveal too much about themselves; they often come across as 'trying too hard' or 'weird'. Most of us struggle to be honest with ourselves! It's not that we don't want to; it's that the mechanics of life don't allow us to. Life is built up of *yes* and *no* seesaws: *yes* you can go shopping; *no* you cannot steal; *yes* you can eat as much as you like; *no* you can't become fat; *yes* you can act crazy for amusement; *no* you can't actually be crazy! Most of us hang out in the middle, in disguises. It's our only way of being ourselves without anyone ever knowing our secrets.

I paid for lunch and we set off again. The afternoon sunshine was beautiful and refreshing. It dried our saturated clothing and took the grind out of the trek. Chomrung was only a few hours away and, despite our conversation earlier, a feeling of contentment had settled over me. I'd somehow managed to put Akio, the Maoists and my rituals to the back of my mind, perhaps by thinking about turning back to Pokhara the next day. Mani wouldn't be pleased if I cut the trek short. It would mean less money for him, but with the threat that hung over us, I didn't think it was an unreasonable request.

There were three of them, two guys and a girl, all equipped with strong English accents. We were about one hour from Chomrung when we bumped into them. They were taking a short break and had found some rocks to sit on. As we passed them one of the guys spoke. 'Hello, mate, you're Irish, aren't you?'

'Yes.' I stopped and looked back. 'Which part of England are you from, then?' Two could play at that, though I had had the advantage of hearing the guy speak.

The girl cut in, 'Oh, we're all from London.'

'Cool. How'd you know I was Irish?'

'You look Irish,' the first guy replied.

I wasn't sure how to take that so I decided to cut the chat and continue trekking. 'Alright then. Sure I'll see you all in Chomrung!'

We walked for about half an hour before things changed. Mani and I didn't realise we were in a race until I heard a loud voice beeping us from behind. Looking back down the path I was surprised to see the three trekkers only metres away from us.

'Hey, look Mani,' I said loudly, acknowledging the challenge. 'Some loafers are hanging around behind us!'

'Come on, Irish, you're not getting tired now are you?'

I laughed. There was no malice in his words as he passed.

'Just thought I'd let you catch up!' I called jovially after him. 'Wouldn't want you to feel like you got annihilated.'

The other two in the group passed us, also beeping as they walked.

'Come on, Mani, we have to speed up!' As soon as I'd spoken I knew it was wrong. I shouldn't be pressuring a sick man. The competitive side of me had galloped ahead.

'Is it a compete?'

I nodded.

'Okay,' he said. 'We try be champion!'

The English travelled at a healthy speed and within minutes were slipping out of view. Already it looked like I'd have to be noble in defeat.

'You see three people?' Mani stopped and pointed ahead. Was he trying to rub our defeat in? The trio had disappeared.

'No, I can't see them, they're too fast for us!'

Mani turned to face me with a cunning look.

'What are you thinking?'

'Today I think maybe we are lucky.' It was good to see Mani shake out of his nervousness, to see him scheming up a plan.

'Come!' he beckoned and, instead of continuing along the track, he veered to the left, into the depths of the forest. Not only was there no longer a path to follow, but we were climbing uphill again, something we hadn't had to do for most of the afternoon.

'Where are we going?' I shouted.

Mani looked back at me with a cheeky grin. 'The track, it go round hill.' He drew a semicircle in the air with his finger. 'But we, we go over hill, come out same point, maybe I think, faster!'

Ah! I acknowledged, thrilling to the challenge. 'Mani! I like your style, my man, I like your style.'

He didn't understand the words but he saw my satisfaction. We continued upward, and in no time at all were over the ascending section and heading down the hill. But there was no sign of the track, Chomrung or the three Brits.

'Are we lost?'

'Lost? No, look over there.' Mani pointed. The path was only metres below us, camouflaged by trees. After days of trekking, everything was looking similar!

Mani suddenly became excited, like a child in anticipation of a new toy. Laughing in a high-pitched tone and jumping slightly on the spot, he gestured towards further down the track. There they were, the three of them unaware of our presence, hurriedly walking directly into our view. Mani let out another burst of laughter.

'Ssshh,' I instructed cheerfully. 'They'll hear us.'

'We have to hurry.' He was tugging my arm and again leading the way. We were in the hot seat now.

Ahead, the track took another turn while our route remained straight. It wasn't long until we were separated from them again. I could see why people didn't generally walk this way: low-hanging trees and prickly branches, along with the uneven ground, made trekking very difficult.

'Nearly there,' Mani signalled back at me, his spirits still elated.

Minutes later the denseness of the forest lessened. Soon we entered a clearing through which Chomrung could be seen in the distance.

'*Yes*!' I clenched my fist in victory. 'We've got them beat.'

'Not yet, still much hard walking, not win so fast!'

As usual, Mani was right. When we rejoined the path, I saw that although we were about fifteen minutes from glory, we still had a staircase to climb, not unlike the first day's three thousand steps to Ulleri.

'Come on,' I yelled boldly, 'we can do this.'

There was no sign of the other three but it wouldn't be long until they caught up.

Step after step, we drew closer and closer to Chomrung. Our energies were sucked almost dry, our will to win challenged by the simple desire to sit down. It was only a short distance, but there was no denying the drastic strain on our bodies.

'They're in front of us!' The voice came from behind and it could only be one of the three Brits. Neither

Mani nor I looked back. The voice sounded distant, we still had a chance.

'Come on, Mani, we can beat them!' He was staggering upwards.

'We're catching up, Irish!' The voice sounded closer. They had made some ground.

Mani stumbled slightly, then regained his footing. He was breathing heavily and his body was arching over, weighed down by the heavy backpack.

'Looks like you're slowing up there, Irish.'

I looked back. Suddenly they were right behind us.

'Only, one, two, three —' he was counting the steps that separated us '— ten, *eleven* steps away from you, Irish.' Mani looked back now too, exhausted.

'Come on, Mani.' I put a hand underneath the base of the backpack so that I held half the weight that was on his shoulders. 'Let's show those guys who can trek the fastest.'

The words seemed to jolt Mani back into life. Step by step suddenly became two-step after two-step. I could hear the breathing of the three behind us, they were maintaining a steady chase at our heels but Mani and I were energised.

About a hundred steps to go. We passed by a number of teahouses. But until we reached the sign saying '*Welcome To Chomrung*' the contest wouldn't be over.

My legs felt as though gravity was dragging them down by the ankles. Ten steps to go! The last stretch is supposed to be the easiest — but it's a lie! Those last ten steps were torture.

'We did it!' I cried as we passed underneath a welcoming banner and collapsed onto the ground in a tired heap. 'We did it!'

I looked up at Mani, who was gazing back upon the steps, with a triumphant grin painted across his face.

'I think maybe we did it very good!'

Mani's words were cheerful and, looking down the steps myself, I saw why. 'Come on, you lazy bastards!' I shouted to the trio, who'd found themselves a place to rest about fifty steps below. They took defeat admirably, raising a middle finger to us, which, in the spirit of all good contests, I returned with satisfaction. What a victory!

11. Card sharks and ghosts

Chomrung was another sign-in post, another point of entry. I produced my permit and signed my name in the trekking register. It was surprisingly comforting — adding my signature to the list of other visitors. Then Mani and I made our way to our guesthouse, the Fishtail.

As I plunged onto the hard mattress, I had never felt so relieved. The pains eased from my body and the day's events played back enjoyably in my head; I was pleased.

My room was smaller than earlier ones I'd found myself in, but it could have been a cupboard and I would have been happy. I lay there — just resting on my back and staring upwards. Should I have a shower or not? The water would probably be freezing ...

Faces from back home, familiar faces of my family and my friends, were hidden in between the splinters of decaying wood and mould in the ceiling. I wondered, if I were to describe to someone what my imagination found in the woodwork above, would they see it as well? It's the strange thing about being away, especially when you leave suddenly like I did, almost everything sparks a memory. Perhaps in this case it was remorse, too, about disappearing, or maybe just homesickness, but almost everything I looked at evoked an image or an emotion.

Once again, looking up I found myself wondering what everyone back home would be doing right now? It was five in the evening in Nepal, so it would be morning in Ireland — they'd all be waking up! Actually not Mam and Dad; they'd have been up already. More than likely they'd be sitting in the kitchen, talking about work or the mortgage. A good night's sleep for them now was about six hours; usually they'd be lucky to get five.

'Look at us two old fogies and we're up before you lot in the morning and asleep after you at night!' Dad couldn't understand how his children could sleep so long. 'We'd have half a day's work done before you lot would show your heads.'

I needed a distraction from remembering home. Quickly I rummaged through the backpack, found my damp and overused towel and, with a heave, dragged my sore body out of the room and towards the shower next door.

When I knocked, a voice called, 'Just a minute, finishing up!'

I knew immediately who it was. When the door opened, all I could do was smile.

'You might have beaten us, Irish, but I beat you to the shower!'

I nodded cheerfully. 'Ah, I'll give you that much. So what's your name?'

'George. What about you?'

'Sean. Good to meet you.' I shook his hand. 'Pity you guys couldn't keep up.'

George wagged his finger at me. 'I don't know how you did it,' he grinned, 'but there's something not right about how you and the little man beat us!'

'We're just too fast!' I replied smugly and closed the shower door behind me with a definite thud. There's nothing more satisfying than winning against a neighbouring country. I'm sure George would have felt the same if the roles had been reversed.

The water was surprisingly warm and felt great, my

muscles loosened, my body relaxed and soon the day washed off me. It was another chilly evening so I dressed in warm clothes before making my way to the dining area. The view from there was spectacular. Below the room was the countryside we'd just passed through and above were majestic mountains.

'It's something else, isn't it?' Her voice, behind me, was warm and friendly.

'I'm Jess, George's sister.' She approached and shook my hand. 'He told me your name is Sean.' Jess spoke in a thick cockney accent, but she looked delicate and regal.

'Yeah, that's right,' I replied.

Jess sat down at the table with me. She had gentle honest eyes, long dark brown hair; her face was nicely bronzed and she had a pleasant, engaging smile. She brought with her only herself, no disguises, and I felt none of my usual awkwardness when meeting people for the first time.

'Do you smoke?' Jess slid a cigarette from a box and waved it in my direction.

'Nah, never really took to them. Work away yourself though.'

'Don't mind if I do.' Lighting the cigarette and putting it in her mouth, Jess sucked in an voracious drag — it seemed to be just what she needed, and the expression on her face said it all.

'So how long have you been trekking for?' It was the standard question, but it was conversation.

'Only one day.' She took another drag. 'We came directly here from Pokhara. Decided against Ghorepani because of the Maoists — not that I'm worried about the Maoists, mind, but it's better to be safe than sorry. What about you?'

'This is my fourth day. I did go by Ghorepani —' I paused for effect '— and I met the Maoists.'

She didn't seem impressed, more interested in her own story. 'Yes, Eric wanted to go through Ghorepani — he's the other bloke, you haven't met him yet — but George and I didn't like the idea.' She began to laugh. 'Can you imagine our parents' reaction if they got a message that George and I had been abducted and killed by the Maoists? They'd be shouting, "They were what? — killed by mice?"'

I smiled out of obligation. She was a strange girl, Jess, certainly confident. As I listened to her talk about her family, her friends, the people of Nepal, the hair dye she recently got, in fact a multitude of different topics, I found myself wondering if she had an off

switch. She clearly loved to talk. It was refreshing to
see somebody self-assured and honest.

'So who's your little man, the guy who was carrying
your bag?'

'Ask him yourself, he's behind you.'

Mani had just entered the room. He was washed
and fresh looking and his still-wet hair was brushed
back flat to his head.

'Ah, now Mani feel good,' he exclaimed with a
smile, slapping his hands optimistically together and
making his way towards us.

Jess rose from her seat and stopped him.

'Wait a minute, stay there.' She gestured to him.
'How tall are you?' Poor Mani didn't know what was
going on, especially when Jess asked him to stand with
his feet flat to the ground, then pressed her back
against his.

'Sean, who's the tallest?'

Jess looked like a giant compared to Mani, and her
glee was uproarious. She was a live wire. Mani
looked startled too, but the pair seemed to hit it off
after she told him that great goods came in small
parcels.

'Thank God for that,' she continued, 'or women
would have no fun, if you know what I mean!'

The menu here was as limited as elsewhere. There was, however, a chicken dish, and I ordered it excitedly, relieved to have the chance to eat something other than *dal bhat* or noodles. George and Eric had come in and, settling down, we reviewed the day's race.

George didn't resemble Jess in any way. He was heavy-set, ginger-haired and rosy-cheeked. He also had a slight upper-class accent and was a little choosier with his words than his sister. As for Eric, he had your typical pot-head university look, slightly grubby in appearance and spoke with the drawl that comes with two or three joints of an evening. He also seemed slightly feminine. It wouldn't have surprised me if he had feelings for George, although I couldn't imagine George returning them. Either way, all three were good company and, as the conversation became more relaxed, I found out that Eric and George were final-year history students at Cambridge, while Jess, who had opted against college, was a store manager in a food market in central London.

'I hate working in a bloody store. I should have gone to college, got a degree, and shacked up with some rich bloke. I could have been rightly set up.'

'What's stopping you from shacking up with a rich

bloke now?' Eric seemed to utter the words in slow motion.

'It's impossible,' she said. 'What rich bloke will be shopping in No Frills Food Market?'

'You never know,' I put in. 'Rich guys are tight as hell.' Jess contemplated this. 'Anyway,' I continued, 'what do you want a rich guy for? Where's the happiness in that?'

'Don't get her started,' ordered George.

'I'll tell you why.' Jess was energised.

'Uh-oh, too late!'

'The reason why I want a rich bloke is because there's no such thing as love, there's just sex. Couples say they're falling in love but that's because they've got a bloody good sex life, probably experimenting and everything. But the minute his lad goes limp or she gets bored, the relationship goes down the drain. I bet if you asked any psychologist why couples break up, they'd tell you it was because of sex. And therefore, when people say they love each other, what they're really saying is that they love having *sex* with each other!' She took a breath. 'So, what I'm saying is, since it's just about sex, I may as well aim for a rich bloke and set myself up, rather than be stuck with some poor bloke who can't afford fish and chips on a Friday night! Anyway, rich blokes are better in the sack because they get it more often and have more practice.'

She certainly had a way of explaining things. The conversation stopped with the arrival of food. Not mine, however.

'Your chicken not ready yet!' The owner pointed towards a lit-up area outside the dining room, where a young boy was chasing after a wild chicken.

'Is that my chicken?' I asked surprised.

'Yes, but first we must catch!'

'Can I try?' I don't know what made me ask. The words just fell from my lips, and before I knew it I was out in the garden standing in front of a wild chicken who'd trapped itself between two walls.

'Go on, Irish, it's a piece of cake,' shouted George.

It should have been a piece of cake; the chicken had nowhere to run. Slowly I approached the fowl, its tiny head bobbing in every direction.

'Just sit still,' I whispered. 'I'm not going to harm you — well, maybe a little.' Soon I was within touching distance of the chicken. Surely it was all over. I crouched down and reached out my arms towards it. Suddenly, as though somebody had just tipped the bird off, it panicked, pecked at my hand and dashed under my legs. I turned swiftly and dived after it. My body thudded on the hard ground like a ton of bricks.

'I've got you!' I shouted.

Two Nepalese kids cackled hysterically and pointed. I knew what they were signalling: the damn thing had gotten away.

'Ah, maybe you have better luck next time, maybe *dal bhat* tonight?' The owner was grinning.

I hobbled back into the dining area. Mani couldn't control himself. Tears of laughter streamed down his face. Well, perhaps my pecked hand and sore body were worth seeing that!

'Can't even catch a chicken?' It was a great opportunity for George to give me a serve. It *was* very funny. What made me even consider chasing around after a chook? Ah well, all in the spirit of good fun. 'It was a pretty fast chicken,' I replied. 'You should give it a go, George!'

'No, Irish, the only chicks I go after are the human type and they've normally got bigger breasts!'

The chicken had pecked my hand sharply and blood steadily trickled out. Since I had some time to wait for my *dal bhat* I decided to go to the bathroom and wipe it with a piece of paper. I found the outhouse located at the side of the guesthouse, out of reach of any light.

The quiet darkness there felt eerie. Uncomfortably I grabbed a piece of toilet paper in the dimness. As I started back towards the dining room, a bang from behind made me look back. There was nothing there, just shadows and, beyond that, darkness. I turned away, but just like in a movie, at the last instant, something caught my eye. Quickly I turned back again.

It couldn't be.

Scanning and walking, I desperately tried to confirm what had caught my eye. But there was nothing there — Akio wasn't there. I could have sworn I'd caught a glimpse of him when I turned away. After a few more moments' looking around, I gave up and headed back to the dining room, rattled.

I had made a mental pact with myself not to think about Akio, about what might have happened to him. If he returned to my consciousness I'd have to submit to mind-numbing rituals. And I just couldn't. I took a few deep breaths and rejoined the group.

Sitting down again, I clenched my fists and pointed my thumbs in the air, keeping my arms below the tabletop. Everybody had finished eating, and though my *dal bhat* had arrived during my absence, I had a prayer to complete. With the others absorbed in asking Mani advice about trekking, I had the space I needed, and once done I turned from my consuming thoughts and consumed food instead.

'Anyone fancy a game of cards?' I asked brightly. There was a general chorus of agreement, and we decided to play twenty-one. Just what I needed to keep myself occupied. Mani seemed excited too, although he hadn't played before.

I showed Mani what each card was worth and how the ace could act as a one or an eleven. 'Now if you don't have twenty-one you can ask for an extra card, but if your score goes over, you lose.'

'Mani understand, we play!' He was anxious and interested, both. I carefully dealt cards to everyone at the table, and they studied their hands.

'Hit me,' said George. I drew him a card.

'*Hit me*?' quizzed Mani.

'It means,' explained Jess, 'he wants another card — it's a different way of saying that!'

'Oh.' Mani pouted, probably not entirely convinced a fight would not break out.

'Hit me again!' I threw George another card. 'Shit, I bust.' He threw his cards onto the table, displaying a twenty-two score.

'Alright, what about you, Eric?' I continued around the table.

'I'll stick.'

Jess looked over at Mani. '*Stick*, it means that he doesn't want any more cards! He's happy with what he's got!'

Mani nodded his head. It was hard to know if he understood what she was saying; the expression on his face was blank, slightly confused. Still he didn't question further.

'Hit me!' signalled Jess.

'Feeling lucky?' I threw her a card.

'I'm always lucky.' She looked at her hand. 'Ah, well, what the hell, hit me again.'

I threw her another card.

'Fuck!' she blurted. 'Pardon my French, one bloody number too much. I'm as bad as my blooming brother.'

'Not so lucky today, eh!' I turned to face Mani. 'Alright, what would you like?'

Mani stared intensely at his cards. I waited, content to be busy, my mind at ease once again.

'I want —' Mani paused and glanced over at Jess for encouragement — 'one hit!'

'Very good, Mini!' she exclaimed.

'His name is Mani,' corrected George.

'Whatever! You've always got to bloody well correct me, don't you?' Jess threw her brother a dirty look. I giggled to myself at the familiar bickering between siblings.

Mani examined the new card he'd been given. His face lit up.

'Maybe I think, Mani want another hit!'

'Alright, here goes!' I threw him another card.

Mani could hardly sit down, he was so excited. 'Maybe one more hit!' he exclaimed. Looking at the fifth card, Mani calmed down — he was taking a moment to count the numbers in his head. Then his face lit up once again. 'Mani, stick, me stick!'

Mani couldn't contain his excitement. He gazed around the table at everybody as though he had some fantastic secret that he might soon share with us all.

I turned my cards over, revealing a king and a four.

'Alright, I've got fourteen, I'll take another card.' Turning a fresh card over showed a five.

'Okay, banker sticks, what have you both got?'

Eric was the first to turn over his cards; he too had nineteen.

'Sorry, Eric, banker gets one extra, so my score's twenty — you lose!'

'That's not right, is it?'

'No, he's right. Banker always gets to use an extra one if they want to,' supported George.

'What a load of rubbish,' moaned Eric, as he pushed his cards away in disgust.

Mani interrupted, he couldn't contain himself any longer. 'Mani winner, Mani winner.'

'What have you got?' I asked him.

Like a veteran card shark, Mani produced his cards one by one, first a king, then an ace. He stopped for effect, then continued again. His third card was an eight.

'That's nineteen. I'm sorry, Mini, but unless you have two more aces up your sleeve, you're not the winner!' Jess had to get her twopence worth in.

Mani smiled back at her.

'Mani is winner!' Released from his grasp, the last two cards fell to the table triumphantly — an ace of clubs and an ace of diamonds.

'Oh my God, that's fantastic,' I exclaimed, cheering Mani on. 'What a brilliant hand!' The other three, seeing how much it meant to Mani, cheered him on too.

We weren't playing for money but still he looked like he'd just won the lottery. 'Maybe now Mani's not so unlucky any more!'

His words showed us a simple man who longed a stroke of good luck. It didn't have to come in the form of great wealth, or even as the wife that he was yet to marry; it just had to be something positive. On this day it was extraordinary 'beginner's luck'. In the next hour we played twenty hands, and to everyone's amazement, Mani won each one of them.

When at last we had had enough and the coolness of the night air was becoming too much to bear, we broke for the night. I stayed a few minutes longer with Mani.

'You were very lucky tonight!' I cheered.

'Ah, tonight was very good night for Mani … Maybe —' he pointed at himself, '— maybe best night.' But then his smile faded, replaced by a look of distant resignation.

'Sometimes,' he continued, 'life not so kind, bring many sad days!' And he smiled again, out of innate optimism, it seemed, more than anything else. 'Thank you for this game. I will remember, maybe when I have children I will teach.'

'No problem, Mani.' I put a hand on his shoulder. 'It was my pleasure. You take it easy, don't stay up all night.'

I made a move towards the door and Mani's voice halted me.

'You remember lady in Ghorepani teahouse — Jagan?' He spoke quietly, almost secretively.

I turned to face him once again and saw he had his head bowed; he seemed deep in thought. 'Yes. I don't think I'll ever forget anything about that teahouse.'

'She is not so young. Have children already.'

'Yes,' I said as he paused.

'I like Jagan.' Mani looked up to meet my gaze. His face was serious and his eyes seemed to be calling for my encouragement.

'That's great,' I replied enthusiastically. She seemed like a lovely woman. Does she like you?'

Mani considered the question for a moment. 'I think yes. We very good friends. For long time now I come to her teahouse.'

I smiled. 'The answer is simple. You should try to win her heart.'

'Marry?' Mani clearly liked the prospect.

I shrugged lightly. 'Why not? Better to marry somebody you like than somebody you don't even know.'

Mani nodded his head approvingly. 'I think you right. Maybe next time I go to Ghorepani I talk to her about marry. Maybe she come with me to your country!'

'Maybe,' I chuckled.

With that, our discussion ended and I left Mani for the evening. On my way to bed I passed by the room of the three Brits, a waft of hash smoke drifted out from within. I smiled to myself.

I don't think I was more than five minutes in bed before I fell asleep. No thoughts came to mind, no rituals, my mind was relaxed. I think Mani's happiness must have been the sedative I needed.

12. *Something terrible*

The morning arrived in blackness. Clouds hung like vultures over the countryside and from them pounded buckets of rain. I shook my head despairingly as I peered out through my door. Oh shit, this was going to be a bitch of a day.

Unenthusiastically, I headed downstairs for breakfast. There was no shelter so I walked speedily. The rain was icy cold as it hit my skin. Near the dining area, the wife and children of the owner were standing unsheltered in the rain, huddled together, heads buried deep into their chests. The woman raised her head only slightly to me.

'You should get in out of the rain!' I said. Confusingly, there was no response from the family.

I went on, keen to get out of the rain myself. But something was terribly wrong.

Three Nepalese men stood at the door of the dining area, staring inside, obstructing my view.

'You should not go inside!' said one of the men, seeing me coming. He raised a hand to stop me.

'What's going on? Is something wrong with the owner? Where is he? Let me inside!' I tried all this — but still could see nothing past the three of them.

'This is not a place for you now. It is best you do not come in.'

They were insistent, but I couldn't walk away. What was the commotion about? I worried for the owner's young family.

I pushed hard past the three men. They tugged on my clothing, dragging me back — but then, with a swift change in direction, I found an opening through their barricade. I shot from between them into the room. Inside, the owner was on his knees, crying. Lying before him, lifeless, was Mani.

Oh my God! Oh shit!

'What did you do?' I shouted and lunged towards the owner.

He turned to look at me. His stricken face was flushed and his eyes full with tears. Before I could reach him, the three other men grappled me back. Then, as they loosened their grip, realisation began to sink in.

Oh Mani. I just can't believe this …

Mani's eyes were open: the pain he'd experienced before he died was marked on his face. The poor man had passed away in sheer agony.

'He was like my brother,' the owner cried, as he rose to his feet. How many times had I heard about that about Mani? He came towards me, tears flowing freely from his eyes, his body trembling. I put my arms out, around him, and he accepted the embrace. The grief that came over me was extraordinary.

Mani's small frame looked so helpless. A pool of blood surrounded the lower part of his body; he'd bled from the inside out. Oh the poor guy, he didn't deserve this. Not Mani, he didn't deserve this. Tears began to fall from my eyes and suddenly I released the owner from my embrace. Without thinking, I fell and grabbed hold of Mani's shoulders and pulled him towards me.

'I'm sorry Mani,' I moaned as I hugged him. 'I'm sorry this had to happen to you.' From behind me I could hear the owner bawling, and behind him the quiet whispers of the three men as they watched.

How stupid I felt. How selfish and irresponsible. *You knew he was sick. You could have forced the issue and put a stop to the trek, but you were too interested in yourself and your own stupid prayers.*

'Dear Holy God, please protect Mam, Dad, John, Sarah and Sam, Benji and Rusty, all my friends and relatives and everybody who really needs God's help, especially please help Mani now, look after him, look after him better than you did when he was alive!'

The last line left my mouth aggressively, with rage, and while my mind was demanding that I start again, I refused to until I was convinced the message was received loud and clear.

'Did you hear me?' I stared at the sky beyond the window. 'Are you reading me loud and clear?'

Eventually I began over again, each new start a failure, each one facing the same difficulties. The men behind me had gone silent; were they listening to my recitals? Finally I lowered Mani's body back to the ground and, taking one last look at him, I stormed out of the room, past the men, and across the unsheltered walkway. Rain and anger — a desperate day.

'I'm sorry,' I called to the huddled family. I raised my hands dejectedly. 'I'm so sorry.' Chomrung was a large village. I just kept walking.

I could feel my body tensing up, unable to respond to the finger rituals, the feet rituals, the 'always looking up' ritual. It was all coming at me at once and there was nothing I could do. I felt boxed in, suffocated.

Eventually I stopped under a tree half a kilometre from the guesthouse and about two hundred steps below. Mani's place of death seemed to tower above, at the top of the hill. I thumped my fist against the hard wooden trunk of the tree and, almost as violently, grabbed at a leech that had settled on me and threw it off into the distance.

From India I had rung home for the first time since being away — it was long overdue. And now it seemed a very long time ago. Mam had answered.

'Hello, Mam. It's Sean!'

Silence had followed, and then I heard Mam break down. She wasn't able to speak to me, her words falling short in the sobbing.

'We thought you were —' she cried — 'dead, and no one knew — why didn't you call, why didn't you —'

Dad took the phone. He was more composed, but I could hear emotion in his voice. 'So where are you. I'll come pick you up?' he finally asked.

'India.'

'India! What the hell are you doing off over there?'

I tried to explain — it was something that I had to do, something I had no control over — but even I would have thought I was full of shit.

Mam had begun to cry louder when she heard where I was. She must have hoped I was just around the corner in a public phone box.

As we hung up that day Mam's parting words were, 'Please, just come home. We love you, Sean, please come home.' But I hadn't.

The rain in Chomrung was getting heavier; it roused me, made me a little more alert than before. I knew I couldn't stay away from the guesthouse forever, but I was afraid.

Reluctantly I made my way back up the hill.

The oddest things came to mind as I walked. I found myself thinking about a hole in Mani's shorts which I'd noticed on one of the climbs. It wasn't a particularly big hole, probably the work of a moth some evening. The significance of it, though, was that Mani couldn't afford another pair; more than likely he'd have to either mend them or just make do. In Mani's life, a simple thing like a hole in his shorts was an issue. He never knew wealth, he never knew success, his life started and ended in hardship. Now it broke my heart to think about it.

Dear Holy God …

No! The prayers had begun again — they hadn't been halted for very long.

The dining area was filled with people when I arrived back: the three Brits, the owner and his family, the men who'd tried to prevent me from seeing what was inside. All of them stood in a quiet circle around Mani's body. I remained outside, unseen.

I fidgeted with my hands, rubbing them irritably one over the other, my mind compelling me to wipe off whatever thoughts surfaced through them. Niggling reproach by niggling reproach they were emerging, and with them a mixture of anger, frustration and fear. I decided that I couldn't stay in this place, I hadn't the strength in me.

In my room I gathered my belongings. Throwing the backpack upon my shoulders I found the straps too tight for me. Mani must have altered them for his own comfort. I loosened the straps and then almost immediately tightened them again — I couldn't do it! I knew I had to loosen them, but each time I tried it felt like I was disengaging from Mani — leaving him alone. It took eleven attempts before I finally succeeded.

As fast as I could, I left the room and walked away, out onto the track. I wanted to look back but I couldn't. It was too hard. Instead I prayed aloud as I walked, maintaining continuous focus directly ahead.

But none of the prayers were working, so I repeated them at top speed, trying desperately to put an end to the torture.

The rain made walking a chore, but I maintained a steady, fast pace. It wasn't long before Chomrung was hidden in the distance and I was suddenly quite alone, still headed towards Machhapuchhare Base camp.

I must have walked for two hours before I finally took a break. I had already passed through two small villages but the thought of being among people had pushed me on. My resting point now was on a large decaying tree trunk, deep beneath the welcoming umbrella of a huge forest. I was out of breath; the track had been almost all vertical, other than the brief downhill section within Chomrung village. Up ahead, it didn't look as though the going would ease anytime soon. I sighed.

'You told him that he'd be okay,' I said to myself. 'You told him that there was nothing wrong with him.'

Other thoughts started flooding in.

Can you imagine what the family would think if they knew the real reason why you left home?

'This isn't the same thing,' I shouted aloud. 'I never thought anything like that with Mani, for Godsake. Why do I always have to go through this?'

I looked around to see if there was anyone who could overhear me. Still there was nobody on the track.

You thought about killing people!

'Go stuff yourself, I did not and I didn't about Mani either.

'I was worried for people, that's why I left Ireland. Nothing else, worry, and that was all! People are allowed to be worried!'

Mam and Dad, family ... sleeping ... suffocating ... stabbing ... poisoning ... The words streamed, jumbled up, nothing concrete, just a combination of painful images. I pressed my hands tight against my forehead but the thoughts only continued to attack. Then I found myself blinking my eyes in intervals of seven, each burst requiring the same perfection as did the prayers that continued rattling away in my head. A recorder in my brain would have picked up at least seven voices all speaking at the same time, all competing with one another for my full attention. At the same time I fidgeted away with my hands.

My body needed this rest but it was better to keep moving — any distraction from the rituals. I rose to my feet once again, struggling under the load of the backpack. Something in this reminded me of a camping trip Dad had taken us kids on when we were little. I remembered thinking at the time how strong he was.

'Sanction, sanctuary, sanctimonious ...'

The words left my mouth instinctively, a defensive mechanism against anything harmful. I hadn't done this in years! The word 'Satan' had once surfaced in my head for no apparent reason, and so I had had to say other words that were similar but counteractive — otherwise people I loved would be harmed. But this ritual had long ago faded from my repertoire! Why had it, too, come back now? I shook my head irritably.

'Come on, no more of this bullshit!'

Thoughts of my sister Sarah floated through my mind —

'Rapture! Raison! Reason!'

It had happened again! This incantation came from a time I'd heard the word 'rape' in my mind. Yes, this was how it had always come in the past, I would think of somebody and then at the back of my mind I would hear some awful word. Sometimes it felt as though my mind had a vendetta against *me*, as though it couldn't stand to have me feeling happy. If I were thinking something pleasant about somebody it would throw in some word like 'cancer', 'rape', 'Satan', 'murder', 'stabbing'. In my twisted logic I believed that since I was thinking of loved ones at the same time as such words were circling about in my head, these people were no doubt going to be harmed in some manner and it would be all my fault, if I didn't do something soon. The antidote, it seemed, was to replace the word or words with other ones that were similar — but positive. Back then, I was replacing words at least fifty times a day.

'Okay,' I began to speak to myself now, 'what the hell is going on with me?' The forest stayed silent.

'*Rapture, raison, reason*, what the hell is that? What does it mean? It means nothing, it means — fuck all!' I was getting angrier by the moment. All I wanted to do was punch something, the voice inside my head if that was possible.

'I'm not listening to you, you can go screw yourself because I'm on my way to the base camp and nothing's stopping me. Not Mani's death, not fucking Akio, and especially not my fucking head!'

The words echoed and quickly faded away, swallowed up by the dense overgrowth of greenery. I set out on the trek again, eyes ahead, mind concentrating hard on blocking out any thoughts, any rituals. But I was concentrating too hard.

'Ah shit,' I cried as I felt the ground below me give way. I hadn't noticed that I was walking so close to the edge. Now it was too late.

My right leg slipped first and with it went my balance. Before I knew it I was rolling down a steep hillside, bashing into tree branches, frantically trying to grab hold of anything that might save me. Tumbling.

The sight of the sky was followed by the sound of a crack. Then there was nothing.

13. Serena

The beach was pitch black but a dog I'd befriended was following me so I felt secure. There was music coming from down beside the moonlit sea — four people singing, and a guitar for accompaniment.

I don't believe it!

It was Serena, strumming the guitar. She was in mid-song as I approached, but realising who it was she sprang up to her feet and threw her arms around me in a warm embrace.

'Serena! I can't believe it. It's good to see you.'

'You too, look at you!' she laughed.

'I met Sean in Varanasi; we chased a dead woman through the streets,' she explained to the group she was with.

I'd drowned my sorrows after my call to Mam

earlier that day and was now too drunk to remember their names. I managed to take in that they were all 'great friends', even though she had met them just hours before while taking a stroll along the ocean. She described it in such a relaxed manner that bonding on the beach, it seemed, was a common event around here.

'You met in Varanasi?' said a curly haired guy with a groan. 'That's a hole of a place. Everyone with their hands out, pleading for something. I couldn't handle it.'

Serena threw a sharp look in his direction but it didn't seem to faze him. I took Serena for a giver not a taker.

'Still, I got to see some wicked bonfires,' he continued. 'They sure send off their dead in a blaze!'

'Come on, who's up for a song?' Serena interrupted, picking up the guitar once again. 'Can you play?' she whispered in my ear.

I took the guitar in my hands. Though it had been a while since I had last played or sung, drunk or sober, I generally performed well. This was where playing by ear was good: while a trained musician might need sheet music to get them through a song, a self-taught musician can always wing it.

I plucked firstly on the E string. The guitar was out of tune, I could tell that. Carefully I started to tune the it, plucking the strings and getting my fingers warmed up on the neck.

'What sort of song is that?' laughed one of the blokes.

'This is what they call —' I stopped for effect '— "Tuning the Guitar".' Serena let out a burst of laughter and rested a hand on my knee.

Finally I was satisfied the guitar was in tune and I put my fingers in place for a B minor strum. I began 'Hotel California' and as I played and sang I felt alive and invincible. It was like being reunited with an old friend you'd never really wanted to part from.

There was applause when I finished and the group began to call it a night. 'My God, man, you've got some voice on you ...'

'Wow! Who the hell are you? Are you like a professional muso or something?' And they drifted away down the beach.

After a while Serena and I were alone. Finding her again like this was more than I'd hoped for. 'What happened to you in Varanasi? You just vanished into thin air!' I said to her at last.

'I didn't vanish, you lost me!' Her eyes were glowing under the moonlit night and her smile was electric. She bent down to pick up the guitar, which I had laid down on the sand, and together we started to walk along the beach.

'I looked all over for you but couldn't find you anywhere.'

Serena laughed gently. 'When we were running through the streets, somehow I managed to take a wrong turn …'

The conversation continued, lively then murmuring. It was a strange walk, underlined with desires which both us seemed to be avoiding. We must have stayed on that beach for nearly three hours before one of us took the initiative.

I wanted Serena to lead the way rather than me. With any other girl I would have tried it on long before then, but Serena had caught me in a different way and I didn't want any dumb move by me to interfere with what was already a great thing.

She began to kiss me. Soon we were undressing each other. And there on the night beach we began devouring one another's bodies.

As I ran my fingers over her breasts and continued down between her legs, my head filled with how utterly stunning she was. We made love that night beneath the moonlit sky, beside the gentle hush of the sea — no inhibitions, both consumed by our every movement. The world no longer existed. When at last we had exhausted ourselves, we lay naked in the sand until eventually we fell asleep, Serena's head resting upon my outstretched arm.

When I awoke as the sun began to rise the next morning we were in exactly the same position.

Serena woke with a shudder. 'Oh my God!' She reached for her underwear and began dressing. 'How'd we sleep so long?'

The early morning sun was gentle and warming. Within minutes we'd dressed. There was an initial awkwardness, but back at my beach hut we undressed again and picked up where we'd left off the night before.

We remained there for most of that day and the next, mainly talking. 'You've got a lot going on in your head, Sean.' Serena had known me for less time than anyone else, but seemed to understand me so much better. She knew that I worried a lot, she knew that I struggled to sleep. She even knew that something had driven me away from Ireland. Her knowing felt good.

We enjoyed a meal in a local restaurant and then took a lazy walk along the beach. Daytime soon became night, and as we sat watching the sunset I was more at peace than ever before.

'You know I'm going tomorrow?'

In a way I wasn't surprised. 'Why tomorrow?' I asked, trying hard to conceal my disappointment.

'I've already booked my flight. I'm heading back to Delhi and from there it's either home or Nepal, I don't know which!'

'Where in Nepal?'

'Perhaps back to Pokhara. It's heavenly!'

There is an unspoken rule about travelling; it's something you pick up on quite fast. Everybody is on their own retreat, whether it be world discovery, self-discovery or simply a case of running away. Whatever the type, travellers all have one thing in common: they're all on solo missions. Even when people travel in groups, each person is on their own quest. Some people go crazy when they travel; they do every mad thing they've wanted to do back home but never felt confident or free enough to do. Then there are others who relax, totally backtrack and unwind, commit to nothing and avoid any sort of interaction. There's a world of different scenarios: shy girls going wild and shagging every man they meet; men sleeping with prostitutes; people eating dog or cat or whatever animal is on the menu; thrill-seekers, drug-takers, troublemakers; the list goes on.

The main thing is that for everybody nothing is stationary; what happens comes and goes, and everybody's always moving on.

Serena and I had been intimate but, like all travellers, she was on her journey and I was on mine. Saying she was leaving soon meant exactly that, and her plans wouldn't involve me. We both knew it. But when it came to saying goodbye, it was harder for me in many ways than leaving home had been.

'You know,' she said, 'I've a feeling we're going to meet again. There's something kind of right about you and me.'

'Absolutely. I'll email you. We'll stay in touch.'

'We have to make sure we find each other again!'

'Come to Ireland, meet me there!'

'No, you come to Australia!' she laughed.

I didn't want our time to end, and I looked for something solid to work towards.

'I'll tell you what. When is your birthday?'

'November thirtieth.'

'Alright, that's about two months away. If we haven't bumped into each other again, I'll make my way to Oz and I'll be standing at your front door singing "Hotel California".'

She laughed. 'That's a deal!'

We kissed. Neither of us wanted to let go. Everything had come to an end so fast.

Serena's taxi pulled away down the mucky main road of Palolem and moments later she was out of sight. And once again out of my life.

14. *A blast from the past*

'Sean, you wake, you wake!'

The words filtered in and out of my head. It was some time before I realised that somebody was trying to rouse me. Finally I opened my eyes.

Everything was blurry at first, a mismatch of green and grey. The back of my head throbbed.

A face came into view, unclear. He was standing over me with the light behind his head. I couldn't quite distinguish him at first. His voice, however, was familiar.

'*Akio*? Is that you?' I forced my aching body to sit up.

'Yes, it is me, Sean. You okay, Sean?'

His voice was comforting to hear and, as my eyesight returned, a familiar face was exactly what I needed — even if it was Akio's.

'Ah, I think you not-o watch what you were doing, you fall like how I did.' Akio laughed slightly, and then sighed as he watched me explore the back of my head with my fingers. 'Oh very painful, your head not look so good-o.'

The back of my head was matted with dried blood. So how long had I been unconscious?

'You very lucky, your head must be very strong.'

Akio was right. I'd landed against a huge boulder, the protruding edge of which had taken part of my fall. Blood marked the spot. How the hell was I not dead?

I sat dazed for a while, in shock. Nothing particular went through my mind. Just waves of disbelief and disorientation. Akio remained silent also, giving me time. Then one thought came, overpoweringly: If I hadn't survived the fall, I'd never see Serena again.

Tears began to fall from my eyes. 'I can't believe … I was nearly killed!'

I looked up to the huge sky. Akio remained silent, unmoved; but I was in disarray. Rituals, prayers, thoughts; instead of protecting me, they'd nearly killed me.

I left home because of damn rituals! My family, the people that I love most — the demands are killing me!

As distraught and foolish as I was, I saw one thing clearly: enough is enough.

Akio took a mouthful of water from his flask. There was something odd about his appearance. He looked perfectly healthy! Not a cut or a bruise in sight. He even had his backpack strapped on his shoulders, although I'd have sworn he hadn't had it when I'd watched him being chased by the Maoists.

He must have got away! Or maybe it wasn't him? Maybe I still wasn't seeing or hearing right?

'What are you doing here?' I said, conscious of the uneasiness in my voice. 'How'd you get here? I thought you were dead. I thought the Maoists had killed you.'

'Not dead, I escaped. They shoot but Akio much too fast for stupid Maoists!' He laughed again, smug.

'Too fast!' I was confused. 'I watched you being chased, and they had you cornered.' While Akio had been a welcome voice earlier, now, realising that he was actually here, felt eerie. My head hurt badly.

'You need to rest, I think,' said Akio. Then he lowered his head. 'Anyhow, I not-o want to talk about it, very frightening.'

'Akio, tell me.'

It was all becoming clearer now. I remembered how Akio hadn't paid the Maoists, how angry I was that he'd put us all at risk.

And Mani. Poor Mani. All that had happened at Chomrung came crashing back on me. Why, in the last days of his life, had Mani had to meet up with somebody like Akio?

'No,' replied Akio. 'There is nothing to talk about. I escape Maoists and I find you. Nothing else is important. You should be happy that I find you!'

Amazingly, having survived my fall, I could feel myself getting annoyed with Akio again!

'Look at me,' I said dully. 'Mani died this morning.'

Akio's face fell. 'Mani, he is dead?' His voice was low. 'How?'

'His stomach. He'd been having pains since I started the trek with him. Probably had them before then too, I don't know.' I reflected for a moment, my mind slightly tingling for a ritual that I denied it. 'I didn't think he was as sick as he was. I don't think he did either. The poor sod was dying all along.'

Akio's eyes filled up with sorrow. He turned away. Why was he so upset, I wondered, he hardly even knew the guy.

'Did you,' he asked quietly, 'pray for him?'

What? Praying and religion were the last things I thought would be of any concern to Akio.

He turned to face me and repeated the question.

'Did you pray for him?'

'Yes,' I answered, slightly shaken. 'Yes, of course I did.' I calmed myself again. 'Why do you ask? Are you a religious person, Akio?'

Akio's demeanour was disturbing; his eyes were cold and empty, blank and expressionless. They gave away something dark, unsettling, and abruptly I felt frightened to be with him.

'I not-o religious, but I think that you are. Maybe you the reason why Mani die!'

My mouth fell open. What the hell?

Akio stood over me again, like an interrogator this time.

'Maybe if I stay with you — ' he pointed a finger down at me — 'I die too. You not so good-o in the head.'

'Wait a minute! Who are you to talk to me like that? There's nothing wrong with my head. You're the one who's got a screw loose.'

'Not me,' Akio sneered. 'I not the one who is praying all the time. You say same prayer all the time. You not good-o in your head. You crazy.'

He had witnessed something when we were in Ulleri, but I didn't think I was bad enough back then for him to have thought I was crackers. I tried to rise to my feet to confront him, but the pain in my head dragged me back, forced me to remain where I was.

'If I could get up I'd knock you out, Akio. You're nothing but a prick. You've been that way since I met you.'

Akio wasn't bothered. He just stared back at me with cold intensity.

'I hear you when you asleep after you fall down here — you talk all the time. Saying prayers. I hear you say that you not-o kill Mani. And —' Akio shook his head as though he were utterly repelled by me — 'you say evil things just like you the devil.'

I was dumbstruck; I couldn't believe what I was hearing.

'Me, the devil!'

'You! Why you think so horrible about people? You want to harm everyone? Your family too?'

I was appalled.

'Horrible things, my family? What are you talking about? I would never wish any harm to my family!'

As the last words left my mouth I suddenly realised what I must have been saying when I was unconscious.

Both of us were silent. Tears began to well in my eyes. I saw times spent with my family, happy times. I wiped my eyes but the tears continued to fall. Akio just looked at me, waiting.

'I've never hurt anyone and I never wanted to harm my family. I was always frightened for them!' The words left my mouth in a sob. 'I've always prayed, always worried that something was going to happen to people, anyone, especially my family. If I didn't wash my hands properly, something bad would happen; if I didn't pray properly, something bad would happen; if I didn't rub my hands properly, something bad would happen. If I didn't do so many different things, something awful would happen. Do you know what that's like, Akio? Do you know what it's fucking like to have to do things over and over and over again to make sure that nothing bad ever happens to anybody?'

Akio looked at me sceptically. He was listening but I didn't think he was hearing exactly what I was saying.

'*It's hell*!' I cried at the top of my voice. 'How do you think you'd feel if you spent every hour of every day reciting things in your head, things that just drove you nuts. You wouldn't be able to handle it, Akio, not you and not anybody else.'

I broke off, the tears streaming down my face. Akio said nothing. He turned away from me again.

'Akio, it's why I left Ireland, why I'm here. I couldn't deal with it any more. All the fucking rituals and prayers were bad enough — but the other stuff, the new stuff, that was just too much.'

The images and the memories were sitting at the front of my mind and they were as terrifying as before. 'Visions, awful visions of my family dying suddenly, my friends being murdered. It was terrifying. I couldn't even sleep at home any more. I was scared beyond belief that during the night something would happen to them all.'

It was a relief to be speaking about everything aloud.

'Things got worse and worse and worse.' I spoke slowly. 'I couldn't sleep any more, thoughts would circle in my head and I would have to perform ritual after ritual to make sure that everybody would be okay. But still the images were terrifying. And I started to ask myself, why was I thinking such things about my family? Was I worried for them or was I willing terrible things to happen to them?

'My family are my life, I would do anything for them. I had no choice but to leave.' I took a deep breath. 'I figured that the further away I was from everyone, the less danger I would be to them. One morning I just packed my bags and took the first flight out of Ireland — didn't tell anyone where I was going or why. Who would understand anyway?'

This was the first time I'd actually confessed all this. Now, hearing it, I heard the stupidity of it all too. How stupid must Akio have thought I was.

'But nothing change!' Akio's words were harsh but true. 'You still sick-o in the head. You dangerous man! You need to be stopped before you hurt more.' Quickly he bent down and grabbed something from the ground. As he rose again, the object in his right hand came clearly into view.

'No! Akio, please don't.' The words left my mouth in desperation.

'Please, Akio, please don't, please don't —'

Akio lunged towards me, his right arm swinging. A gasp left my lips as I tried to protect myself. But it was hopeless. The rock in his hand smashed hard against the side of my head and threw me backwards. I grappled blindly with him, trying to release the weapon from his hand — but he freed his arm. A second blow made contact and then I couldn't move.

I lay flat on my back staring into the sky. Suddenly Akio came into view again, a vicious look on his face. He raised his arm again and delivered a final blow to my face, and everything went blank.

15. *Time to go*

Was I dead? The sounds of birds and wind and trees all around me were familiar but at first I was unable to move. The pain in my head was intense. Then, slowly, I opened one eye and, surprised by what I saw, the other. I wasn't dead, I was exactly where I'd been before, lying out in the middle of the cold forest. I was still alive. He hadn't killed me. Akio hadn't killed me.

Akio — where was he?

Fear shot through me and I jumped to my feet. Dread of Akio eclipsed the pain and I leapt punching the air in every direction. If Akio was near, I would kill him. I swore to myself that I would kill him. But he was nowhere in sight.

'Akio, you bastard. Come out you fucking wanker!' I screamed at the top of my lungs.

I stood still and listened carefully.

'Where are you?' I shouted, then listened again. Still nothing! There was no sign of him, and something told me that he was no longer near.

I gave up the fight and fell to my knees then curled to my side on the forest floor. For what seemed like hours I cradled myself. I was numb and defenceless.

Where did everything go wrong?

Why am I the way that I am?

How could Akio do that to me?

I could hear birds overhead and now the sunlight created an array of lengthening shadows in front of me. Leeches had attached themselves to my leg, and were sucking hard at my blood. But I remained in a daze.

When I became aware that night would soon fall, I rose slowly to my feet. The weight of the backpack sat heavily on my weary, damaged frame. I wiped my wet eyes and took a final look at this place, at what I'd just escaped from.

'Holy God —' I gazed upwards, slightly nervous. 'Holy God, this is hard for me to say and I know that you know it is!' I paused. Who was I talking to?

I continued because I knew that I had to. Whether there was somebody up there listening or whether it was just to myself, the words had to be spoken. 'Holy God, I don't even know if you exist. I don't know if anything I ever say to you makes a bit of difference to anybody. You know I'm not religious and, to be honest, I don't believe that you'd listen to half of the crap I say, even if you do exist.'

I took another deep breath. 'Look, the fact is that, well, I'm walking out of this forest and — and you're staying, you're not coming with me.' It felt as though a load was being lifted from my shoulders. 'This is it, this is my last prayer. If you're really up there, if you're really listening to me, then I know you don't need to hear from me a million times a day. I wouldn't like to hear from somebody a million times a day talking about wrecking their head. I trust you, I know you'll look after us all, you always have and …' This was the hardest thing I had to say. 'And then again, if you don't exist at all, then we'll all have to look after ourselves!'

I looked in every direction. I took in the forest, the patches of sky, the fading light, the place where I'd fallen, and finally I looked up again.

'Okay, I've got to go. I'll be seeing you.'

Turning around I took my first step back up the hill I'd fallen down. It was hard, like walking into the unknown. I didn't hesitate though. My head ached and my stomach growled with hunger but I quickened my pace. Not looking back, I climbed, each step more confident than the last. Thoughts circled around my head — guilt, worries, Akio, niggling pressures to perform rituals. I just let them circle and continued upwards. I didn't fight the thoughts and I didn't appease them either. I let them come and go. And I wasn't frightened by them. I knew that what I was doing was the right thing.

My family would want me to do this. They don't want me suffering the way I do. It's time I started living my life.

At last I surfaced from beneath a dense patch of greenery and was greeted by the path. My heart lifted. This was living. I shouted it to the world. 'This is what life is all about!'

Turning to the left, I hurried. There was about an hour of daylight remaining. And there was something I had to do. Stripes of red crossed the sky as the blue started to fade with the setting sun. The green of my surroundings gradually became a fuzzy grey and my eyes struggled in the pending blackness.

*   *   *

Through the aches and the throbbing and the thin light of my torch, thoughts continued to play at me but I refused to give in. I wouldn't pray, I wouldn't respond. Somewhere deep within I knew that forever more it was probably going to be this way. That this was something that would never leave me, something that I would spend the rest of my life fighting.

I passed through a small village where candlelit houses greeted my eyes kindly, but still I continued on. There was no more hard climbing, just up and down as usual — until my destination came into view.

I turned a bend and there it was, a collection of dimly lit households, scattered at the top of the distant hill. It felt good to see Chomrung again, even if it was still about an hour away.

The final leg of walking was uphill the entire way and my body was weakening under the weight of the backpack. I paused and started off again. But at last it was too hard and I did what I should have done at the bottom: I unbuckled the backpack and let it fall to the ground. I heard it tumbling down the stone steps I'd just climbed, but I didn't look back to see where it landed. Instead I began to run. Tripping occasionally, I forced myself up the steep staircase, the teahouse directly in view. Everything seemed vivid. At last

I reached the teahouse, where I fell to my knees, exhausted. Yet I felt more alive than ever before.

'Thank you,' I cried at the top of my lungs. 'Thank you!'

The owner of the teahouse helped me into the dining room. I was laughing, and strangely enough he seemed to understand.

'What happened to you?' he asked, seeing the blood on my head. 'You need somebody to fix your head, it look very bad!'

'No, I'll be okay. I want to see Mani, where is Mani?'

The owner stared at me, confused for a second, and then gave a gentle smile.

'We have prepared him in one of the rooms. Tomorrow he leave for Pokhara!'

'Tonight I want to stay with Mani. Can you show me where he is?'

Outside one of the upstairs rooms, we stopped for a second.

'You sure, you okay?'

'Yes. I'm meant to be here.'

I wasn't nervous about entering the room, but just in case I reminded myself of who it was I was going to see: Mani, a soft and gentle man who wouldn't harm a fly.

And indeed, there was nothing to be nervous about. There were two single beds in the room; Mani was laid out on one of them. A candle flickered warmly on a side table. They had draped his entire body in a white cotton cloth, leaving only his face exposed. He looked totally at peace with himself and, strange as it sounded, I felt happy for him; he seemed to be in the right place.

'You were a good man, Mani, a very good man.' Bending down, I kissed his forehead. It was as if he might suddenly wake and speak, he looked so like a man in a deep sleep.

'You're not going to have that wife after all, Mani.' I nodded my head in sorrow. 'I suppose it just wasn't meant to be. Maybe you weren't so lucky after all.'

Now tiredness caught up with me. I lay down on the other bed.

'Things have a way of working themselves out, Mani. I only knew you for a short while but the memory of you will stay with me forever.' I was silent for a moment.

'Goodnight, Mani,' I whispered drowsily and smiled. Then I fell asleep, not a thought in my head, my mind at rest.

16. Leaving

Morning arrived and I awoke early. I was lying on my side, facing Mani.

'Good morning, Mani,' I whispered. 'Today we both leave for home!'

Four of us carried Mani's body from Chomrung back to Birethanti. No one spoke for the entire trip, the three other men concerning themselves with the job at hand, and at all times mourning. This was a spiritual journey and Mani, I felt, would have been happy to be thought of with such love.

Images and words continued to press me, but I held strong to my decision. My demons were not going to just vanish overnight. Giving anything up is like turning your back on everything you think you know and understand. You can train yourself to live without it, but you can never forget it, and for as long as you live it still remains a part of you.

Going downhill in the final stage of our journey was more arduous than going up. Along the way people stepped aside to let us pass, but nobody asked what had happened to Mani.

By five hours into the second day, we were close to the end. We had dropped considerably in altitude and the countryside was becoming busier with houses and people. Soon Birethanti came into view. I think all of us became excited and we walked a little faster.

Om, Mani's trekking boss and cousin, was there to greet us. He was in floods of tears as we arrived, and embraced me for a few moments. 'You good man,' he whispered gently, 'you very good man.'

Mani was back with his own people and our journey together had run its distance. Om and the three men would continue with his body to Pokhara. I placed a farewell hand on Mani's forehead and then, with a heavy heart, finally turned aside. I didn't look back to see the men carrying Mani away. It was hard to believe this was the end. I hadn't reached base camp, but it felt like I had reached a great deal further. After one last look back along the track, I headed towards Nayapul and the main road.

As I sat in the first taxi I could find, I felt a mixture of joy, sorrow and disbelief. In silence, I recalled the various events of the trek. It seemed like I'd been away for such a long time. Serena came back into my mind; I really hoped I'd see her again.

The driver looked up and into his mirror at me.

'Did you meet the Maoist?'

The Maoists! 'Yes!' I answered.

'Oh, you very lucky.'

Lucky? If anything they were the start of all the problems.

'You very lucky to still be alive,' the driver continued. 'One boy, Japanese, Maoist kill, nearly five days ago.'

I felt my face go pale with fright.

'What?'

The driver passed a newspaper over to me. It was in English, but still I couldn't believe what I saw. In the centre of the page was a picture of Akio, and below it, one of his family arriving in Nepal to take his body back to Japan.

'Very sad,' the driver sighed. 'And very sad for Nepal. I think not many tourist come now for trekking, not good for business.'

I was hardly listening.

Five days ago? That would have been when I saw Akio being chased. How could that be?

After a few minutes of pure confusion, I smiled to myself. 'Unbelievable,' I said. 'Unbelievable.'

I looked up at the driver. 'Have you got a radio in this car?'

'Yes, you want to hear some music?'

'Yes,' I replied. 'And turn it up as loud as you can!'